MW00883550

Sweet Pickle Books
47 Orchard Street
New York, NY 10002

# TOM SPARKS

The Lost Coast

*"There's a light on yonder mountain*
*and it's calling me to shine*
*There's a girl over by the water fountain*
*and she's asking to be mine*
*And Jesus is standing in the doorway*
*in a buckskin jacket, boots and spurs so fine*
*He says, 'We need you son tonight up in*
*Dodge City*
*'Cause there's just too many outlaws*
*trying to work the same line."*


*"Oh tumbleweed keep rollin',*
*he just roams from town to town*
*It ain't easy for a half-breed kid*
*to try and settle down*
*Tumbleweed keep rollin',*
*he can't find no place to rest*
*Yeah the desert wind blows tumbleweed*
*like some spirit of the west."*

# THE
# LOST COAST

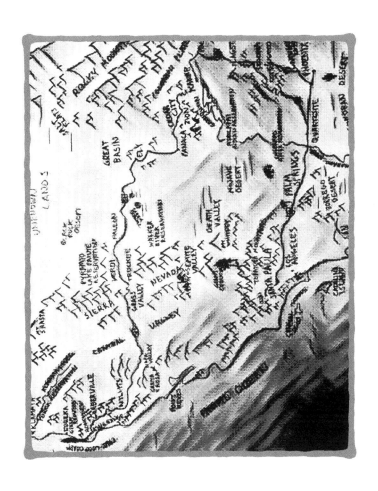

*A great aunt is teaching her great nephew about life.
"A fight is going on inside me," she said to the boy. "It
is a terrible fight and it is between two mountain lions.
One is evil – he is anger, envy, sorrow, regret, greed,
arrogance, self-pity, guilt, resentment, inferiority, lies,
false pride, superiority, and ego."*

*She continued, "The other is good – he is joy,
peace, love, hope, serenity, humility, kindness,
benevolence, empathy, generosity, truth, compassion,
and faith. The same fight is going on inside you – and
inside every other person, too."*

*The great nephew thought about it for a
minute and then asked his aunt, "Which mountain
lion will win?"*

*The great aunt simply replied, "The one you
feed."*

- Native American parable

MILLIONS UPON MILLIONS of years ago, undivided Cretaceous marine sedimentary and metamorphic rocks of the North American Plate were lifted sharply upward by Mendocino Triple Junction interactions with the Pacific Plate and the southern tip of the Juan de Fuca Plate, sometimes known as the Gorda Plate; creating a coastal ridge forming a drainage divide parallel to the Pacific Ocean. Thousands of years ago this land was inhabited by the Yurok people who thrived there until the gold rush in the 1850's, after which disease and massacres decreased their numbers by more than seventy-five percent. The area was named the 'Lost Coast' after it experienced still more depopulation in the 1930's, as it was considered too expensive for state highway or county road builders to establish routes through the severe terrain. Even one hundred years later it remained by a wide margin, the most undeveloped and remote portion of the California coastline making it the perfect place to hide stuff.

"Bout time Jimmy," Popeye said in a wheezy voice as he laid in bed, barely clinging to life. Jim Deere stepped forward and closed the door behind him. Boyishly handsome, with bronze skin, tousled black hair, and the build of an olympic sprinter, Jim's eyes betrayed his smile and revealed his grief. He wore a t-shirt and jeans that smacked of the road, and a brown leather jacket was draped over his right shoulder as he sat down in a chair near the headboard.

"Sorry Prez, Snod was hasslin me."

"Them boys seem to think that I got a trove of money stashed away, he was  pressin me too, all afternoon, but I never told em nothing." He sighed and his rosy skin turned a whiter shade of pale. "They'll never find it anyway."

Jim leaned in closer. "What do you mean?" He noticed that Popeye had become very still, until suddenly the old man sprang to attention with a jolt.

"I hid it far away Jimmy!"

He couldn't tell if the man's already suspect mental condition had worsened from his sudden turn of health and decrepit state, or if he was trying to convey something serious, then the big familiar smile returned, which put Jim's mind more at ease.

"You hid what?"

He had heard the rumors over the years, just like everybody else, that Popeye had a large amount of cash stowed away somewhere, but like everyone else, he never knew the details, or if it was actually true.

"It's all taken care of, all the money," the man said in a raspy whisper as he lifted his head toward him. "I hid it. Hidden treasure Jimmy!" He laughed and out of habit raised his hand to cover his teeth as he always did. With his mouth closed he was quite handsome, although with his bushy salt and pepper beard and a black patch covering his lazy eye, he had the appearance of a pirate, and in many ways, that's what he was.

Popeye Rush was the president of the Santa Paula chapter of the Iron Raiders motorcycle club, and the undisputed leader of one of the most notorious one-percenter biker gangs in the Southwest. In recent years, he was more of a figurehead than anything else, but to Jim, he was a kind old man and he loved him dearly.

"Try not to talk so much," Jim said as he became fearful that the life in Popeye's used up body was fading fast. "Maybe I should go get help."

He should've been in a hospital, but he was a stubborn soul and it was his wish that if was going to die, he was going to die at home. Jim couldn't blame him. He lived in a quaint Victorian style house at the base of a hill in the Santa Clara River Valley. It was a beautiful idyllic setting, isolated and quiet, adjacent to avocado and lemon orchards with the only neighbors being the occasional black bear that would roam down from the Topatopa Mountains. It was as good a place as any for an old outlaw to die on his own terms.

"I need you to do somethin for me," Popeye said with some urgency in his grizzled voice as he grabbed Jim's arm.

He looked straight into Popeye's lone good eye. "Yeah, sure, whatever you want."

"My daughter," he said as his face softened. "She don't like me very much." He turned and looked at the blue sky through the window and listened to the scrub jays chirp for a long moment before he spoke again. "A man wants to know that he left somethin behind in this world. She deserves a whole lot better than what I gave her."

"What you want me to do Prez?"

He pointed to the desk across the room with a shaking finger. "Go into that top drawer. There's an envelope, you'll see."

Jim got up and did as he was told. The envelope was obvious, and right where he said it would be. It was marked only with the name 'Samantha', and he grabbed it and brought it to him.

"I took that out of the safe last night. I want you to find my daughter and make sure she gets that." He nodded at the envelope, still in Jim's hand.

"You could give it to her yourself," Jim said with encouragement, but knowing in his heart that Popeye would probably never leave his bed again.

"You have to do it," Popeye said, his voice now becoming very weak. He shimmied up into a sitting position. Still in his clothes, he reached into his pocket and pulled out his wallet. After some strain, he took out a photograph and gave it to Jim. When he spoke again, sorrow was heavy in his voice. "Her name's Sam, she lives in Arizona, she's about your age now."

Jim Deere looked at the photograph with care, drawing his lips together and raising his eyebrows before putting it on the nightstand and turning back to Popeye, sensing the importance of what he was saying.

"How will I find her?" he asked, suddenly quite intrigued although still confused by the way Popeye was confiding in him so intimately at this late stage in the game.

"In the town of Jerome, there's a place called the Spirit Room, ask for Tea Cup."

"Tea Cup?"

"Yeah, Tea Cup."

Jim studied the envelope. "What is it?"

"It's what Snod's been lookin for, it's what they've all been lookin for. It's the map to my treasure!" he said with surprising loudness, before coughing. "A treasure map!" he added with childlike enthusiasm after clearing his throat. He leaned as best he could toward Jim and lowered his voice back into a secretive whisper. "Promise me, you'll find her and give it to her, make sure she gets my treasure."

Jim stared hard at the man, seeing the sincerity and earnestness that was evident in his eye. "I promise."

He slithered deeper into his bed and uttered under his breath, "Diego."

Jim angled himself closer. "What?"

"She goes by her mother's name, Diego."

"Okay," Jim said with a somber nod.

"You've turned into a fine young man Jimmy, just stay away from the booze and you'll be okay. Remember, it is a great advantage not to drink. I trust you and I love you like family. I'm not proud of what I done, but maybe some good can come out of it." With great effort he reached into the drawer of the night stand and pulled out a thick roll of cash. "Take this, for your trouble," he said, handing it to Jim and watching him look at it like it was more money than he had ever seen. "Don't be like me Jimmy, and don't trust them other guys, you gotta get outta here, leave this behind, don't wait…don't wait until it's too late."

Before Jim could protest being given so much money he noticed that Popeye's eye had become fixed, and his pale face had become white as snow.

"Prez?" he said in despair as he touched the man's forehead. It wasn't warm. He checked his pulse at the wrist, there was nothing. An awful lump formed in his throat and his eyes began to tingle. He put his jacket on, stuffed the cash in the pocket, and looked around the room to make sure he was as alone as he thought. He sprang to his feet, ran out the door and called for the others.

There were several members of the Iron Raiders motorcycle club hanging around the house as it was well known that their President was on his last legs. A few of them scampered in while Jim stood in the hallway in shock. He didn't need to see anything more, he knew Popeye was gone.

"What you got there Halfbreed, he give that to you or did you take it?" Snod Farkus asked with sneer as he walked right up to Jim.

It took a second to register what Snod was asking, as Jim's mind was still reeling. The roll of cash was hidden away but he hadn't realized he was still holding the envelope, plain as day in his right hand.

"Nothin," Jim said, peering up at Snod as cooly as possible, shoving the envelope into the back pocket of his jeans.

Most guys were scared to death of Snod, but if Jim was he didn't show it. He saw his huge heavily tattooed arms, exposed in his usual cut-off sleeves and black leather vest as a sign of insecurity, rather than something to be intimidated by. As of late, he found it a great strain to be around people like Snod and the Iron Raiders. Their presence perturbed him, and the effort of conversation irritated him. But it was Snod that would undoubtedly take Popeye's place as the new

President of the chapter, and he had always hated Jim with intensity.

Jim attempted to walk around only to have Snod step to his left and block his exit. "Get out of my way," Jim said as he tried his best to act tough.

A menacing smirk formed beneath Snod's dark horseshoe mustache as he stared Jim down. He was a brute of a man, over six feet tall and outweighing Jim by at least 60 pounds. Age 35, he was thick at the waist and a mass of untoned muscle and evenly displaced flab. Glistening chest hair poured out beneath his undersized shirt and seemed to grow sporadically over the entirety of his lobster red sunburnt skin.

"Gimmie that envelope!" Snod yelled, grabbing Jim's arm. "Gimmie gimme gimmie."

"Get off me!" Jim twisted free of Snod's grip, brashly bulled his way around him and scurried toward the front of the house.

Although he hadn't been expecting to receive a deathbed order to track down an estranged daughter, Jim had been preparing to leave the Iron Raiders altogether for some time. Without Popeye there was no reason to stay.

He knew it could be tricky, as leaving an outlaw motorcycle club was easier said than done. He had known men who wanted out before, and he had seen them get their tattoos removed by force with white hot knives, applied repeatedly to their skin until they were so badly burned they often died in the process.

Snod chased, but Jim was too quick. All he could do was watch from the front porch as Jim hopped on his motorcycle and rode away down the dirt driveway like a bat out of hell. A fellow club member named Boone Dix, who was already outside, scratching his back on a wooden post that supported the canopy above, stepped forward.

"Where's Tumbleweed off to in such a hurry?" Boone asked as he looked at the rapidly disappearing comet tail of dust from Jim's bike. To most of the Iron Raiders, Jim was known as Tumbleweed, or Halfbreed or sometimes Pretty Boy. Popeye was one of the only guys who called him by his given name.

"He's got somethin of Popeye's," Snod said, stroking the mustache that hung well below his chin. He squinted, like the wheels in his head needed grease. "He knows somethin. I want you to tag em."

Snod had been increasingly suspicious of the young Jim, and he never liked that he had such a close relationship with Popeye. Popeye often buried large amounts of cash in the ground as he was neurotically fearful of Uncle Sam coming down and freezing his assets and bank accounts, and it angered Snod that the old man had become so secretive about such doings.

Popeye used to brag about his daring Robin-Hood-esque heists, the vast sums of money he had stolen over the years, and his legendary bank robbery, but recently he had shifted silent, sober and reclusive, and in the meantime the Iron Raiders had become insufficiently funded under his leadership.

Some people feared the Mongols and the Hell's Angels, but the Mongols and Hells Angels feared the Iron Raiders, and Snod considered himself responsible for keeping that reputation alive and well. Every time Snod would ask Popeye where all the money was hidden, or what he did with the cash from his biggest scores, Popeye would become coy, dismissive, act insane, or deny such money existed altogether, and the way he seemed to divulge freely to Jim, only served to fuel Snod's rage and his mistrust in his authority. But with Popeye now out of the picture, Snod was free to take matters into his own hands.

"You got it boss," Boone said as he handed Snod a can of beer from a plastic cooler.

"Booney?" Snod said before cracking it open taking a slobbery swig.

"Yeah?"

"You can call me…" He stopped, as his words were interrupted by his own mouth releasing a thunderous belch deep from the bowels of his throat like a frog's croak amplified by a megaphone, powerful enough to blow curls into Boone's whiskers. "You can call me Prez now."

Winding his way up State Route 150 toward Ojai in the gold of the setting sun, sadness hit Jim like a collision. Popeye Rush had been his only true ally. He had known him since he was 10, when Popeye caught him red handed, right in the middle of trying to hot wire Snod's Harley Road King in a tavern parking lot on the northern California coast.

If anyone else in the club had caught a skinny native kid trying to steal one of their bikes, they likely would have beaten him to the brink of death or killed him on the spot, but not Popeye.

What Jim wanted to do more than anything was to pound a drink alone in his trailer, but he was the type of guy who would have beer and wake up on Venice beach with a full beard, and he was not going to let himself forget his promise, or the envelope that he carried, or the picture of the man's daughter. He thought of his assignment of finding her as the perfect excuse to leave the gang and never come back, and drinking himself into oblivion could wait.

He descended into the Ojai Valley and pulled off the two-lane highway onto the unpaved gravel of Strawberry Lane until he arrived at a natural meadow where a 1966 Airstream Caravel was parked. It was a tiny aluminum bubble with a rotting floor and a smattering of dents decorating its exterior, but it was his most commonly used sleeping quarters, and he needed rest if he was going to execute his disappearing act early the next morning.

He stepped off his bike and held the precious envelope as the late June sun disappeared behind the coastal Sierra Madres. He wanted to take a look at the photograph of Sam again, as something in her eyes had captured him, but checking his pockets, front and back, he realized he didn't have it.

His head lowered and his shoulders slumped, remembering he left it on the nightstand back at the house, and he cursed himself for being so stupid and careless. With such a whirlwind of emotions in a short amount of time, he hadn't been thinking clearly.

After kicking the dirt, he went inside the trailer and pulled out his map of the western United States which quickly reinvigorated his spirit. For as long as he could remember Jim had a passion for maps. As a small boy on the rez he would often go to bed, staring for hours at the expanse of the American West, losing himself in the glories of exploration until he fell asleep.

Jerome, Arizona was a small town a few hours north of Phoenix, he guessed a good 500 miles away from where he was now. He ran his finger along the roads and thought again about what the girl in the photograph looked like. He closed his eyes and tried to imagine her as a person and not a picture. He wondered what she was like, or how she would handle receiving the news of her father's death, or how she would react to being given a supposed treasure map of all things.

He figured most guys in his situation would open the envelope and look at it straight away, forget the daughter and go after the money themselves, but he was not going to do that. The best that could be said of him was that he was trustworthy. The worst that could be said, from the perspective of the remaining Iron Raiders, was that he did not represent them nor did his independent lone  rider attitude fit with their herd mentality. He was first and foremost a motorcyclist and a man of the road, and the road was where he felt most at home, not in his trailer or the clubhouses and bars like the rest of them. His purpose for finally joining the club was mostly financial, and because of his love for riding. In the immutability of his surroundings, the unfamiliar towns, the unfamiliar faces, the changing enormity of life and scenery that flew past, he was floundered not by a sense of wonder but by contemptuous bewilderment, for there is nothing mystical to a motorcycle rider unless it be the road itself, which was the muse of his existence and as enigmatic as inevitability.

His mind raced until his trance was broken by the sound of a Harley approaching. He peered through his tattered venetian blinds. It was Boone Dix.

Jim stepped outside.

Boone dismounted, killed his rumbling engine, and removed his doughboy helmet and cordless headphones. He stared up at Jim and said, "Popeye's dead."

Boone was a wiry fellow, five and half feet tall with sunken cheeks and dark knitted eyebrows that made constant demands upon the rest of his face. At his side he wore a wallet chain that looked heavy enough to tip him over.

"I know," Jim said.

"Snod wants to know why you run off so fast, says you got somethin a his."

"I don't got nothin."

Boone snarled. "He's gonna be the new President, you gotta answer ta him just like you answered ta Popeye," he said, hanging his helmet on the ape-hanger handlebars of his beat up Sportster Forty-Eight.

"Yeah well, you ain't him."

"You was the last one to see em alive. The boys and me all wanna know what he said ta you."

"Nothin, he didn't say nothin," Jim said as he thought again about the picture of Popeye's daughter, sitting on the nightstand next to his body.

"Ya see we all a bit confused, being as old Popeye never did seem to mention ta nobody what he done with all his money. He didn't have no wife or no kids so we figure he must have left instructions for us somewhere."

"Well he didn't tell me what he done wit it," Jim said, shifting his weight from one foot to the other. "That why you came all the way out here, just cause you think I know somethin bout his so-called treasure? I'm just the no good halfbreed Tumbleweed remember? Why would the old man tell me anything?"

Boone bristled. He took a step toward Jim's motorcycle, which was parked in front of his.

"Indian Scout," Boone said as he ran his hand along the curvy contours of the bike. It was a magnificent looking machine, although it hadn't always been. When Popeye had first found it, or

21

perhaps stole it, it was in need of serious repairs and Jim had taken great pride in fixing it up, tearing it completely apart and putting it all back together again over the 3 years that he owned it. The result was a unique and beautiful, customized look, with black paint, brown seats, passenger backrest, saddlebags, and chrome everywhere else. Even though it wasn't a Harley-Davidson, it made Boone jealous, based solely on its pristine condition. One of the requirements for club membership was to own a bike that was not only American made, but also displaced at least a thousand cubic centimeters of air-fuel mixture through its engine. Jim's bike was American made, and his displaced eleven-hundred, so he qualified, despite it not being a Harley. "Fitting you the only brother that's got an Indian. You know Popeye never got a bike for nobody cept you."

"So what?"

"That crazy old man had a soft spot for you, so that's why we think he may have told you somethin that he didn't tell no one else, we know there gotta be a map or somethin."

"Sorry to disappoint," Jim said as he placed his hands in the pockets of his jeans and tensed his shoulders.

Boone closed his mouth tight and twitched his poorly groomed van dyke beard and mustache. "Get me a beer Halfbreed."

Jim shrugged, went back inside his trailer to meet Boone's demand for a brew. Jim was still just technically what they call a prospect. That is, a wannabe, or someone who is not yet a full patch member of the motorcycle club, unlike Boone. It would be unheard of for a prospect to refuse a request from a member, and the last thing Jim wanted was to raise any more suspicion than he already had.

Now alone outside, Boone pulled out a small plastic device from his pocket and peeled off a protective coating exposing a heavy duty adhesive. He attached it to Jim's bike deep beneath the rear wheel fender, completely hidden and out of sight. The implement was about the size of a silver dollar, and Boone was no stranger to doing this. He had used the tracker many times before, usually for keeping tabs on hang-arounds suspected of being undercover cops, or on members of rival clubs for various reasons. This was not a widely known practice, but Boone loved gadgetry and it was his specialty.

He stepped away and looked at his phone just as Jim came back out and tossed him a can of Modelo. Boone stared at him like he was trying his best to intimidate him before he placed his phone in his jacket pocket, whipped out a switchblade and stabbed the beer in its side. He shotgunned it down in one long swig and then threw the can on the ground.

"You best be back at the house first thing tomorrow mornin," he said as he flashed a frightening smile of missing teeth. "We gonna have a lot to go over."

"Yeah, I'll be there."

Boone scowled and put the headphones back in his ears, got on his Harley and rode off.

The boisterous sound of a metal bladed Sawzall cutting into a safe rang throughout Popeye's house in the late morning of the following day. With their former leader's body already removed by the coroner, it was decided by Snod to break into the safe, which was something he had been chomping at the bit to do for a long time.

"How's it comin?" Snod yelled as he looked down at the shining bald head of Dice Moya, who was doing the cutting.

"Almost there!" Dice shouted as he gritted his teeth and sunk the powerful saw deeper into the poorly designed metal box. With sparks flying and one last screech, the safe broke in two, and Dice used a crowbar to pry it the rest of the way open.

"Let me see!" Snod said as he bent his knees and lowered himself down for a closer look, eager to investigate what he thought to be inside.

"Nothin," Dice said, dejected.

"Where is it!" Snod screamed. He jolted up and kicked the door of the empty safe with his steel-toed motorcycle boots.

"Look at this Prez," Wille Wheeler said as he noticed the photograph on the small table next to Popeye's bed. He picked it up and handed it to Snod.

Snod scrunched his eyes. "Who's this?" he asked, staring at the picture and scratching his head. "He didn't have no family right, where's Boone?"

"Don't know," Willie said.

"No Tumbleweed neither?" Snod asked as he felt the anger building up inside of him.

"Nah, can't get a hold of him," Wille said, rubbing his hand against his bicep.

"Try em both again and tell em to meet us at church!"

With that, Snod and his fellow posse of compatriots stormed out of the house and blazed down the road on their Harleys, heading for town. Church was an Iron Raiders bar across the tracks from the old Railroad Depot, and it had been the clubhouse for the Santa Paula chapter for many years.

Snod, Wille, and a long haired blonde named George Armstrong, as well as a barrel bodied older fellow called Glub Bubber, backed their bikes into parking spots out front and entered the saloon together like they owned the place, mixing instantly in the sea of leather vests with the familiar black and silver patches on the backs. Full of men, the air was thick and muggy and it smelled a strong mix of body odor, fried Mexican food and hard spirits.

"The usual," Snod said to the bartender Delilah, as he slapped the wooden countertop over and over again like a bongo drum with eager impatience. Delilah was a woman north of 50, with a wavy green wig, thin painted on black eyebrows which made her look a little surprised, and visible neck tattoos. She had been the heart and soul of church from the beginning.

"Ice machine broke again," she said in her usual deadpan voice, although loud enough to be heard above the blaring death metal that dominated the room.

"Lemme axe you a question," Snod said as she brought him a jigger of Mellow Corn. "Did Prez have any next of kin?"

"Prez owes me money," Delilah said. "I told him not to die until he paid off his tab. Never knew a man could rack up such a bill without even drinkin."

"He didn't have no daughter or somethin did he?" Snod asked after guzzling his drink in one quick quaff.

"A daughter?" Delilah asked with a fake eyebrow raised. "Oh yeah Prez got a daughter over in Arizona."

Snod flinched forward. "How you know?"

"He was as tight lipped as they come, but he would talk in his sleep quite a bit."

"I'm gonna need some more information," Snod said as he slid his empty glass toward her.

"You pay off his tab and I'll tell you anything you want," she said in a snarky tone.

"This her?"

Snod showed her the photograph of the girl that Willie had found by the bed.

She leaned in and looked. "Could be."

"Come on, you know Popeye had money stashed away. It's my feelin that if he had a daughter he might have wanted to give it to her and not to the club where it rightfully belongs."

"Well his house is goin to the club, not to no daughter so maybe you should just be grateful for that," Delilah said.

"Sorry I'm late Prez," Boone Dix said as he suddenly appeared from behind.

"Where's Tumbleweed?" Snod asked with a snarl.

Boone shrugged, holding his phone. "I got him all the way past Indio."

"What? Let me see that!" Snod said as he snatched Boone's phone from his hand. He looked at the screen. It indicated that he was on the 10, way out near Joshua Tree. Snod's eyeballs bulged as if a light bulb went off in his head. "Goin to Arizona?"

"Don't know," Boone said. "No need ta wait for em here though."

Snod growled and downed his second whiskey before throwing the glass on the floor as hard as he could, shattering it instantly in a fit of rage.

"Hey!" Delilah screeched. "You owe me a new glass!"

"Everybody listen up!" Snod yelled, unsheathing his Bowie knife and slamming its butt repeatedly against the countertop like a judge's gavel. The music turned off and the crowd went silent as he surveyed the room and prepared for his speech. He addressed church like a preacher. "As you know, we lost a real good man last night. He was our leader, and a man that we could all depend on. We are all going to miss Popeye."

"He was a great man, but what he do with his money?" a fellow member named Stone Graves asked in a booming voice as he sat next to a Turkish guy named Wes Saeed, while a gentle hum of grumbling followed.

"The man was crazy!" Flash Fontana said. "Respect though, rest in peace," he added as he made the sign of the cross on his chest.

Snod whipped out his pistol from the belt at his side and fired a single shot right into Stone Grave's head from a distance of less than twenty feet. He was killed instantly where he sat, his torso teetered and slumped, and the room went silent once again. Wes Saeed's eyeballs looked ready to fall out of his sockets, and  Snod twirled the gun around on his finger like a baton before holstering it in a show of clout. He had their full attention now, and he continued speaking as though nothing happened.

"As for his money and his so-called treasure, we thinks there's a map that seems to be missin, and our good friend Tumbleweed, who was the last one to see old Popeye alive, has run off and is headed east."

"I say we go after him," Glub Bubber grunted with a cautious nod.

"Oh we be going after him. Whatever money Popeye had, he earned it as an Iron Raider, and that money will go back to the club, mark my words. I find out that anybody called and warned Tumbleweed that we comin for em, they gonna end up in Jericho just like brother Graves," Snod squawked, sneering at the body that had just fallen off its chair onto the wooden floor with a dull thud. "That means they don't get their share of the loot!"

Everyone erupted in a cheer and followed Snod's lead in reciting the Iron Raider motto out loud and in unison. "UNDER THE BLACK FLAG WE RIDE, AND THE ROAD SHALL BE OUR EMPIRE!"

The music was then turned back up and the men went back to shooting pool and nursing their drinks, carefully stepping over the dead man that was sprawled out on the floor in a pool of blood for the time being.

"So when we leaving Prez?" Boone Dix asked as he and Snod turned back to Delilah.

"Let me talk to Deli first," Snod said with his face deep in thought. "But we go tonight, avoid the heat."

"You gonna pay me what he owes or what?" Delilah asked.

"If you help me find out what he done with his money, and where his daughter is, I'd pay off what he owes and buy you a brand new ice machine," Snod said with a devilish smirk.

It was so hot that Jim Deere felt as though he might spontaneously combust once he made it to Quartzite, Arizona, about halfway between Los Angeles and his destination. It was a nothing town, encompassed by arid desolation for hundreds of miles in all directions. He stopped at a Love's travel center to rehydrate himself, and stuffed his face with donuts and beef jerky, as his overheated body felt desperate to replenish burned calories and lost salt. He stripped from his black long sleeve shirt and drenched it with water from a rusty sink in the brightly lit gas station restroom and put it back on as he prepared to continue. The desert heat was so intense that it was imperative for him to stay covered and wet as much as possible.

Dripping, yet drying fast in the furnace-like sun, he walked back to the far end of the parking lot where he had put his bike in the small shadow of a creosote bush, seemingly the only shade within a hundred mile radius. Just as he was about to hop back on, he noticed something glittering in the sunlight on the curb next to his kickstand. He was sure it hadn't been there before, as he would have certainly noticed it.

He picked it up. It was heavy and shaped like a small guitar pick, gold with a green gem in the center. He looked around. He was nowhere near anyone, and he didn't know why exactly, but he was beginning to feel as if he was being watched, which made him wonder if he was becoming paranoid. Shaking off that notion, he puzzled over the piece of jewelry. If it was made of gold it would be worth something. He looked around again, pondered briefly about turning it into the clerk in the mini-mart, but thought better of the idea and put it in his saddlebag before firing up his engine.

From there, he exited the 10 and took highway 60 toward Prescott. He looked forward to reaching the peaks to the north of where the Colorado plateau descended into the Sonoran lowlands, as higher elevation was sure to bring cooler temperatures, and anything less than the current 110 degrees would be a welcome improvement.

Despite the scorching weather, it was a beautiful day. Wide open landscape and countless saguaro cacti encompassed him in all directions, and a he saw a hawk take flight from a rocky cliff in the east, mirroring his sense of freedom, sailing solitary in the cerulean sky far above the earth and its swarming freight of gregarious life.

When he reached Jerome the sun was disappearing and he was exhausted, especially after the last 30 miles of tightly wound mountain roads. Jerome was a former copper mining town built spectacularly on a steep bluff that overlooked the Verde Valley. He shifted down into second gear as he rolled through the narrow street, keeping his eyes peeled for the place Popeye told him about.

The town was so small that it wasn't long before he saw an ancient brick building on the corner of a hairpin turn called the Hotel Connor.

At street level it had an entrance marked with the words, 'Spirit Room'. He parked his bike next to the sidewalk, took off his sunglasses and walked in.

The place looked like it could be haunted, as it had eerily maintained the style of it's 19th century old west construction. It was a Thursday evening, and inside, it wasn't too crowded, but there was a lone guitar player in a cowboy hat playing melodic acoustic country music on a corner stage that was drawing mild attention.

"Can I see your ID?" the man behind the bar asked as Jim sat down at a vacant stool near the window. He pulled out his wallet and did as requested after which the bartender asked, "What you want?"

Jim had stripped off his long sleeves once he rode into the mountains and he knew he probably looked a bit bedraggled in his dusty white t-shirt and blue jeans, but surveying the place again, he figured he fit in just fine. He was hungry and very thirsty, but all he said was, "Tea Cup, can I...ask for Tea Cup."

"Tea Cup?" the bartender asked. "We don't serve no..."

"Who askin for Tea Cup?" a lady in the corner of the room interrupted in a powerful voice.

Jim turned his head. She was and older woman with dark brown skin and frizzy grey hair braided into a ponytail that she hung over the front of her left shoulder. She wore a light blue denim tunic dress with a thick white belt and silver buckle around her waist, amplifying her slim, hourglass shape. She had a stern face, yet a hint of kindness shone out from behind her dark brown eyes.

"I am," he said. She approached slowly from behind the bar and looked him up and down.

"What are you Maricopa?" she asked.

Jim was startled by the question. Most people didn't notice that he was part native, the guys in the club mostly called him Halfbreed just because they knew it got under his skin.

"Uhh..Yurok," he said, not expecting the woman to know what he was talking about. "O'loolekweesh," he added with a bashful half smile.

She furrowed her brow. "Alas, poor Yurok... Redwoods?"

"Um, yeah, that's right," Jim said, surprised. "Just uh, well I really don't remember much about it."

He spoke awkwardly like he wanted to change the subject. He knew where he came from, but they weren't pleasant memories. He had grown up on the Yurok reservation in Northern California, but once orphaned he ran away, and had been on his own until Popeye found him.

"You're far away from home," she said.

"I just come from Los Angeles."

"What's your name?"

"Jim, but ah, everyone calls me Tumbleweed."

He decided not to mention the halfbreed part.

She was amused at his nickname when paired together with his appearance. "Haven't been called Tea Cup for years, not since I started drinkin again," she said, as if she could feel his uneasiness. "Who told you that name?"

"Umm..." He paused and cleared his throat. "Popeye Rush ma'am."

She took a step back, frowned, and drew her eyes to the high ceiling. She looked back at him.

"Popeye?" she said as her face melted into a warm smile. "And how is old Popeye?"

"Well, I, I'm sorry to tell you ma'am, but he umm, passed, few days ago."

"Oh...oh no," she said with genuine sadness, placing her hands on the bar. She remained silent for some time. "Did he send you to me?"

"Yes ma'am."

The woman looked at his sun beaten face and arms, and gazed out through the window and saw the Indian motorcycle parked across the street.

"Come on back and we'll talk, I'll get you some water."

Jim followed her to a table in a quiet corner of the room, on the opposite side of the stage, and she served him ice water and a cheeseburger that he devoured before she had a chance to sit down with her metallic mug.

"You seem a little too nice to be a black and silver," she said, referencing the colors of the Iron Raider's patches as she noticed the distinctive smiling skull and crossbones that was tattooed on his forearm.

"I was just a prospect."

"So why you here?"

"I have something from Popeye, somethin I need to give to his daughter."

"Oh, his daughter," she said, taken aback.

"He told me to talk to you, just right before he died. He told me, maybe you could help me find her."

Her eyes narrowed and then softened. "He was too young, he wasn't even 60, how did he go?"

"Don't really know, he was in bad shape for a while I guess. Then he just got real sick...and died in his bed a few days later," he said, his voice growing morose as he felt the sadness rushing up from his chest to his nose and eyes.

"Hmm, never thought he would go out that way," she said before taking a sip from her drink. "You were there, with him when he died?"

"Yeah, I was there."

He reached into his pocket and took out the folded envelope. "I promised him I would give this to her, his daughter I mean, his dying wish," he said as he showed it to her. "Sam Diego."

She stared at him with a peculiar look on her face. "Anybody else know about this?" she asked, taking the envelope and rubbing it between her fingers, as if feeling what might be inside.

"Some might have their suspicions, but they don't know much."

Her expression said she was contemplating whether or not to tell him what she knew. She sighed and took another big sip from her drink and continued to study his eyes. She cleared her throat.

"Haven't seen Samantha in a while. She works at some horse stables out near Sedona, at least last I checked. Trails End Ranch, it's in the Village of Oak Creek, if you know where that is. Village of Old Creeps, as some people call it."

He was astonished that she told him what he needed to know so freely, and he felt like a huge burden was lifted from his shoulders.

"Thank you." He pushed his chair backward, repeating her words in his head over and over, contemplating what to do next. He downed the rest of his water and rose.

"If you find her, bring her back over here, tell her I'd love to say hi sometime," she said rather wistfully. "Or if she has any trouble with what's inside that envelope."

"I will," he said, puzzled as he peered down at her and perceived the loneliness in her eyes. "Trails End Ranch."

"That's right," she said as he turned to go.

He took one step forward before she stopped him and asked, "You got a place to stay tonight?"

"Uh, no."

It was only then that he noticed it was now dark outside. It would be too late to find Sam at this hour, and he felt thoroughly drained from the long ride through the desert anyway.

"The ranch would be closed by now, no need to be in such a hurry. I could put you up in one of our rooms, you could probably do with a shower."

It suddenly hit Jim that he had no place to stay.

"Uh…yeah, okay that sounds good," he said, turning toward her.

"Come on."

She stood, and led him to the back of the room and through a door that brought them to the foot of a wooden staircase.

"What's she like?" he asked as he followed her up to the hotel on the second floor, the boards of the stairs creaking spookily with each step.

"Sam?" she asked with a turn of her head. "She ain't like her father."

After a breakfast of delightfully fluffy buttermilk pancakes and strong black coffee the next morning, Jim got back on his bike and headed into the Verde Valley.

Having looked up the location of the ranch the night before, he followed route 30 toward the small town of Cornville, before taking a left on Beaverhead Flats Road, which connected through a landscape of desert, to the Village of Oak Creek. As he approached his destination he was greeted by the sight of the majestic red orange colors of the famous Bell Rock and Courthouse Butte that dominated the skyline. He was amazed by what he saw. It was breathtakingly beautiful, and the stillness of the scenery had a calming effect.

The Village of Oak Creek was much more of a modern development in comparison to Jerome, and Jim noticed the grandeur of the homes as he passed through, each one appearing bigger than the last. He took a right at one of the roundabouts in town and headed north across a dry wash until he saw the split rail fence of a ranch. He rumbled down a red dirt road through a timber framed entrance and parked his bike near a small building which he assumed to be the office.

There was a sign above the door that read, 'Trails End Ranch Office' which confirmed his assumption.

He didn't see anybody inside, but as he walked in the adobe structure and then out to an open field adjacent to the back face of the building, he saw two women struggling to lead a spirited quarter horse toward the stables.

"No, you've got to be tough with them, don't let them think they can get away with that!" The older woman yelled as she hit the animal hard on the head while the younger woman clasped the bridle. The older woman then turned to see Jim, standing and watching. She had a bleach blonde perm and she wore oversized cat eye sunglasses beneath a white visor. "Can I help you?"

"Yeah, I'm lookin for..." Jim started to say as he gazed more closely at the younger woman. She was dressed like an equestrian, in tall brown leather boots and khaki jeans, but she wore a cowboy style hat that partially covered her face in the starkly contrasting shadows of the mid morning light.

"We don't offer trail rides here," the older woman said. "We serve horse owners only."

Jim was startled by her harshness. He had indeed showered and changed his shirt, albeit into another t-shirt, but he didn't think he looked too bad. Who was she to say he wasn't himself a horse owner?

"I'm looking for Sam Diego," he said, peering at the younger woman again, who instantly lifted her head and looked straight at him.

"She's working," the older woman said as she glowered at the girl before looking back at Jim sourly. "I ask that you do not bother our employees during business hours and I am going to have to ask you to leave."

He was taken aback. Was his appearance so abhorrent and foreign to this woman that she would so quickly and crudely turn him away? He lowered his head and looked back, facing the entrance to the office where he noticed a white Tesla model-X pulling into the dusty parking lot. A young white guy that looked like he came straight from a cologne commercial, stepped out of the vehicle and sauntered in like he was the lord of the tennis club.

"Oh hello Mr. Albinson!" The older woman said in a suddenly cheery voice. "How are you today?"

"Yeah good, just wanted to get a little ride in before my tee time, sorry I didn't call ahead," the man said, in what Jim perceived to be a rather high-pitched and pompous voice. "And to say hi to Sam of course," he added with a smile as he gazed at the younger woman.

"Oh no problem that's just wonderful, Sam will go bring Vanderbilt right out for you," the older woman said, as she with brazen eyes nodded her head up and down at the younger woman.

Jim curled his lip and placed his hands in his pockets as he watched the lady welcome this man with such hospitality, before sulking back to his bike.

A pack of two-dozen or more Iron Raiders buzzed in tight formation down Highway 10 toward Phoenix like a swarm of killer bees. They rode in a precise military-like pattern that seemed an awesome display of power to each and every car they passed at their steady speed of ninety miles per hour.

With a close eye on the tracker which had confirmed Jim's whereabouts, it had been decided to take the 17 north toward the Verde River Valley, instead of route 60, as Snod wanted to discuss things further with his fellow brothers in the valley of the sun. It was late morning, and the troop had been riding through the night. They all converged on an Iron Raider clubhouse on the outskirts of the city, near New River, in a place called Wranglers Roost.

"And you think dis guy Tumbleweed know where Popeye hid his money?" Bronson Barrera, who was the President of the North Phoenix chapter asked Snod in his slight Chicano accent.

"He's just a prospect," Snod said as the two of them drank beer in the spacious and fenceless backyard of the house. Red Dog O'Manbun and Charles 'Meatbone' Bukowski were practicing shooting handguns while riding motorcycles in the distance of the barren desert as the men spoke. "But he was pretty tight with the crazy old man."

"So what you think he has?" Bronson asked.

"I think he got somethin that says where Popeye's treasure is," Snod said, raising his eyebrows up and down almost comically. "I think he has a map."

Bronson chuckled. "Dat treasure is just a legend."

"1992," Snod said in an ominous whisper as he leaned in closer, ignoring the laughter.

"Come on man," Bronson said. "If dat was Popeye we would have found out by now."

"I'm, not so sure."

"Either way don't matter. Popeye collected a lot of cash over the years," Bronson said as he ran his hand over his greasy black hair. "Dat money should go to the club."

"That's what I'm sayin brother."

"If you axe me, Popeye lost his mind…long time ago!" Bronson said with animated panache before wrapping his lips around his long neck beer and tipping it upward.

"You don't think I know it?" Snod said as Boone Dix approached with his phone in hand and a cigarillo dangling from his mouth. Snod turned toward him. "Where's he at now?"

"Looks like, Sedona area, just north of Camp Verde," Boone said as he studied his screen and blew smoke into the hot morning air.

Snod sucked on his beer before turning back to Bronson. "So how bout it, we got permission to do what we gotta do?"

Bronson took off his sunglasses and looked Snod directly in the eye. "You can kill the kid, he only a prospect, and if it true dat Popeye took the money and try to give it to his daughter, then make sure she tell you where de money is first. We'll tail you up there wit de van, I'll talk to Billy."

Snod smiled. "How's the wife?"

"She good, she still a killer, on assignment now."

"Classified?"

"Of course," Bronson said as he put his glasses back on. "Whatever money Popeye had, you got to find it. It your chapter now."

Snod downed the rest of his beer and clutched the bottle like he was going to break it in his bare hand. He looked at Boone. "Tell the boys to start wakin up, we best get movin soon."

Later that evening, Samantha Diego walked out the office doors at the Trail's End Ranch, and saw Jim Deere, waiting in the unpaved parking lot, leaning against his motorcycle. She recognized him from earlier and begrudgingly went toward him.

He was excited to meet her, but he reminded himself that he was there to deliver sad news. He had never told anyone that a member of their family had died before, and he wasn't sure how he was supposed to act so he deliberately forced his mouth into a grim frown, which made him look quite strange.

"You're still here," she said, glaring at him and taking in his appearance. She gazed at him warily, as the expression on his face startled her.

"Yeah, I…I came back and just waited," Jim stammered as he stood up straight. He was nervous. He was also unprepared for her to look the way she did up close and in person, and it was immediately obvious to him that she didn't get her looks from her Dad. "I'm…my name's Jim. I was a friend of your father."

He watched her closely as she bit her lip and eyed him with curiosity. She was still in her equestrian outfit, the same hat and sleeveless white blouse, but now with a small leather handbag draped over her shoulder. She was a few inches shorter than him, but her heeled boots and high-waisted pants seemed to add length to her legs.

"You're Popeye Rush's daughter right?" he asked, just to be certain, still a bit taken aback by her well put together visage. Knowing Popeye, Jim had expected his daughter to be somehow different, not this angel of a young woman, stunning beyond his comprehension and beautiful enough to reduce him to agony.

"I don't know anybody named Popeye," she said, blunt and expressionless.

"You're Sam Diego? Umm, Ronnie's daughter, Ronnie Rush?"

Now he had her attention.

"What do you know about him?"

Jim took a deep breath, slightly distracted by the way her hair was cascading well passed her narrow and petite, yet softened shoulders. He gazed into her eyes. They were unlike any eyes he looked upon before. They were penetrating, dark and mysterious, and behind them there was a ferocity and intelligence that Jim found both dazzling and intimidating, like she could see right through him and already knew what he was about to say.

"I'm sorry, but I come to tell you, that um, he passed away two days ago."

Her face changed. Her eyes gave away her sadness and turned inward upon herself, but she didn't appear to be shocked.

He sighed and took out the envelope from his pocket. "He sent me to give you this, I promised him."

She glared at him with skepticism, but took the envelope and looked at it carefully. Her sight drew down and then back up, and then to the motorcycle behind him.

"You're an Iron Raider aren't you," she said after a long silence.

"I was, I was just a prospect."

"You rode that all the way from California?"

"Yeah." He stepped to the side and looked around the parking lot, unsure of what to do or say next. He put his hands in the back pockets of his jeans and turned toward the west where the sun was beginning to set, giving the still visible Courthouse Butte, even more of an otherworldly glow. He looked back at Sam, and realized she was staring at him. "Sorry, I just, I come a long way to give that to you, I somehow thought there'd be more to it. I weren't expecting it to be so easy to find you."

She placed her weight on one hip. "How did you find me?"

"Tea Cup."

"Tea Cup?"

"Yeah, the lady at the Spirit Room in Jerome," he said as he leaned back against his bike again, trying not to seem as anxious as he felt.

She adjusted her handbag and gave him a side-eyed look. "Paula?"

"I don't know," he said with a shrug. "She knew who you were, your Dad... called her Tea Cup."

Her face brightened ever so slightly. "You talked to her?"

"Yeah, stayed in her hotel last night."

She exhaled, searching for words. "How did he, umm," she started to say before she wavered and cleared her throat. Jim stood back up and noticed that her eyes had become glossy.

"Why don't we uh, go sit down," he suggested, nodding toward a bench that was up near the corral. She wiped her eyes with the back of her finger as gracefully as she could and pulled out sunglasses from her purse and put them on before looking at him again, unsure of what to do with the knowledge that her father was dead, or what to make of the boy standing in front of her.

He was dressed in cowboy boots mostly covered by dusty blue jeans. A perfectly fitting white t-shirt revealed an angular body and broad shoulders. His face was deeply tanned by the sun and a five-o'clock shadow covered a strong jawline. His dark eyes fixated on her in a disarming sort of way and she decided she didn't feel like being alone.

The setting was so peaceful and serene, especially in that twilight hour of the evening. No cars, no freeways, the only sounds being the gentle hum of cicadas and the occasional quiet neighs and whinnies of horses.

"It's beautiful here," Jim said as they walked toward the bench in even stride.

"I am sick of the desert."

"Really, why?"

"Because it's a desert. Everything is hard, nothing is soft, just look around, even the plants have spikes on them," she said, flashing him a hint of a smile, the first time he had seen her do so. "Also, it's a hundred degrees every day," she added, gazing at the rocky landscape. "I'll take the ocean over this."

There was silence as they reached the edge of the corral and sat down on the garden style bench. Restless, Jim ran his hands along his knees while she arched her back and examined him in acute contemplation.

"How well did you know him?" she asked.

He sat up straight. "He was like a…" He hesitated, sensitive that Popeye had perhaps been more of a father to him than he had been to her. "He was a good friend. I didn't have nobody, and he found me when I was a kid, and uh, took me in I guess."

He scolded himself for using such poor grammar as soon as the words left his tongue, as he was painfully conscious of his inarticulateness. He had never spoken to a woman like Sam before, someone whom he thought of as in a much higher class than himself. He imagined that she had grown up with a wealthy mother and a pony, expensive riding lessons and private schooling. He already assumed, upon first resting eyes on her, that a cavernous gap lay between them, himself the halfbreed trailer trash, and she the classy beauty, and the very idea of her made him nervous.

"That's more than he did for me," she said.

"I'm sorry," he said, clearing his throat. The two stared at each other for what Jim felt like was an eternity. She had taken her hat off and her bag was no longer over her shoulder, and he found that her exposed neckline was making him feel even more self-conscious. He tried to think of something else to say to break the awkwardness. "That lady you work with, she don't…" He caught himself. "Doesn't seem very nice."

"She's not."

"You…like working here?"

"No, every day I think of a reason not to quit, but I love horses, and I can barely afford to pay my rent as it is," she said after an annoyed breath. "Although she treats horses so..."   She thought for a moment. "I believe you need to work with the animals, not against them."

"Do you ride?" he asked.

"Yes I do."

"You got a...do you have a horse?"

"I wish, it's too expensive to own," she said. Her gaze relaxed for a moment on his shoulders, his tan skin and young body, spilling over with hardy health and strength. The places that her eyes and mind were going surprised her, and to him, her look made him unconsciously more comfortable in her presence.

She reached into her purse and took out the envelope. She breathed deeply and tried to think of the obvious more somber subject, the reason why this man was here with her in the first place. "Was my father..."

He tried to anticipate what she was trying to ask as she trailed off. "He seemed peaceful, after he talked about you and, knowing I would get that to you," he said with a gesture at the envelope.

She stared at it like it scared her. "I'm going to open it."

She tore through the seal and removed its contents of folded paper. Holding up the first sheet she read it silently like a letter while Jim stayed quiet to give her time and space. He looked up at her again when he heard her gasp and sniffle and noticed that her eyes were filled with tears.

"Hold on a sec," he said as he got up and ran down to his bike. He found his little pack of tissues in one of his saddlebags and jogged back up to bring it to her. Just the sight of him doing this made her smile despite her watery eyes.

"Thanks," she said with a whimper as she took a tissue and brought it to her face. Composing herself, she went to the other paper and looked it over before handing it to him, much to his surprise. "Do you know what this is supposed to mean?"

He studied it. It was a map.

"Yeah, I think I do," he said, placing his hand against his forehead. "It's a map to umm... your inheritance."

"What?"

"As long as I knew your father there was always this kind of legend...rumor that he had a big, final...buried treasure somewhere," he explained as sincerely as he could, realizing his words might sound ridiculous to someone that didn't know Popeye well, even if it was his own daughter.

"The Lost Coast?" She leaned closer to look at the map again. It was a detailed drawing of labeled coastline with a section indicating a dotted line leading to an area marked only as 'The Wishing Tree' next to a depiction of a heart symbol. No other markings were next to where the dotted line ended but in the area surrounding it there were intricate sketches of landmarks, streams, hills and mountains.

"I guess, now we know where," he said, trying to hide his amusement of what Popeye had done. He looked at her blankly. "The Lost Coast is around where your Dad found me, when I was just a kid."

"Weird," she said with a subtly sly look.

"What?"

"The last time I saw him, he and I were there, up by the ocean in California, why did he..." She stopped herself.

"He wanted to leave something for you, he had regrets. Said he hoped that some good would come out of all the things he'd done."

"What is it?"

"Money or, cash I guess, I really don't know."

She looked straight ahead and paused for a moment before turning back to him, biting her lower lip. "Is it blood money or drug money or something?"

"No. I ain't sayin he always earned his money by legal means but...he wasn't an evil man like that."

Her smirk of curiosity turned bitter. "What did he think, this was supposed to make up for, everything?" She folded her arms against her breast and crossed her legs.

"I have no idea what he was thinking, but that's it, there it is, you can do whatever you want with it."

"He was so crazy," she muttered with disgust. She uncrossed her arms and reached for another tissue.

"He was...but he loved you."

Her eyes narrowed at that remark and she balled her hands into fists. "He was not a father to me, I didn't know him."

He sighed, folded the map up and handed it back to her. There was a long pause.

"What do you think you'll do?" he asked finally.

"I don't know." She put the map and the letter back into the envelope and then placed the envelope into her bag.

"Aren't you curious?"

"Of course," she said, standing up. "But I don't even know if it's real, or if…I don't know what I'm supposed to do with this information."

"You should go talk to Tea…Cup."

"My dad didn't know me." She spoke animatedly with her arms. "He didn't know the first thing about me, and now he expects me to chase down, illegal cash or something somewhere halfway across the country?"

"He was a strange man, but I know, he had a good heart."

She took a deep breath, sniffled, and stood still.

"What are you going to do?"

Her question surprised him. Both because she cared enough to ask and because, he really hadn't thought about it. He had been so focused on fulfilling his promise to Popeye that he hadn't the slightest idea of what to do afterward.

"I'm not going back to the Iron Raiders."

"Why not?"

She sat back down next to him.

"Your Dad was the only reason I was there," he said as he watched her slide her hips backward on the bench. Catching himself in a lingering stare he quickly drew his gaze upward. "I want to make my own way, I want a better life than the one I come from."

"Me too," she said, now trying to read his eyes. "I understand that for sure."

His face lit up. He couldn't remember the last time someone had told him that they understood him in such a way. Understood him for wanting something more and something better. He pointed at her purse.

"Whatever that is, he sure wanted you to find it."

"I don't even think my car could make it that far," she said before looking at her phone, which was abruptly illuminating. "It's getting dark, I need to go."

"You gonna be okay?"

She stood up, grabbed her handbag and hat and stared at him, expressionless. "Yeah, to me, he was already dead."

He rose to his feet as well and she stretched out her hand and studied him with interest. Suddenly, she saw him as such a boy as he stood blushing and stammering his thanks that she had received him. That frown of his had dissolved, and his big eyes and crooked smile caused an almost maternal wave of pity to well up in her. Gone was her first impression of the man who startled her in all his raw masculinity. She saw before her only a child who was as internally frightened and lonely as she was, who's hand that she was shaking felt so worked and calloused that it nearly scratched her soft skin.

"It was nice to meet you," was all she said before walking back to her old Honda Del Sol that looked like it had seen better days. He walked behind her and got back on his bike watching as she pulled out of the dusty parking lot, just as the sun was disappearing completely behind Bell Rock.

"It was nice to meet you too Sam," he thought to himself with wistful longing as she drove out of sight.

Jim rode back up to the Spirit Room in Jerome as the night grew dark. It was the only place around that he knew, and he had nowhere else to go.

"How about a beer, stranger?" Tea Cup asked after he took a seat at the bar, on the same barstool next to the front window that he sat in the night before.

A beer sounded very good, but after meeting someone like Sam, Jim felt a strong desire to rid himself of himself, and beer, (he thought) would have the opposite effect. "I'm thinkin about it but a, no, just coffee please," he said with a bashful shrug.

"Smart boy," she said before grabbing the pot behind her and pouring him a cup. "So, tell me all about it."

"I found her."

"And?"

"Could've been worse I suppose," he said as he brought the mug to his nose and took in the ashy, burnt, long since brewed smell.

"She's a nice girl," she said with a smile. "A real cutie pie."

"Yeah," he said as he returned her knowing look. "Popeye he a…"

Jim trailed off as he looked out the window and lost himself in his thoughts for a moment.

"What's next for you?" Tea Cup asked as if she could read his mind.

He turned his head toward her.

"Don't know, maybe I'll head north."

"Why?"

"Just to get away, start over, find some place where you don't need to get patched in to become a member."

"I'll drink to that," she said as she poured herself a shot of something, raised her glass and gulped it down. He halfheartedly smiled before she walked away to help other customers, leaving him to stew. He could start over with a clean slate and go anywhere he wanted, and do anything he wanted. He just didn't know what that was. He thought more about it during the next hour or so, but the feeling he kept returning to, was that he missed Popeye, and he questioned his abilities to move forward on his own.

It was Friday evening, and the Spirit Room was much busier than it had been the night before. He turned around in his seat and saw that a group of young women were sitting at a table and one of them was looking at him, drawing his gaze and flashing him a smile. He smiled back but quickly looked away and toward the stage where a woman with a guitar had started singing an Alison Krauss tune that he recognized. As he listened to the words his mind drifted back to Sam and the feeling of her hand in his. Her palm was so different from his own, like a flower, soft and warm and as light as a snowflake. Her hands reflected her essence, and the softness about her was foreign to him. The minutes passed and he floated off into a dream of longing.

"I keep on waiting for you to come talk to me but you just ain't gonna budge are you," a voice said, jolting him back to reality. It was the young woman who smiled at him earlier. She was blonde and slim with black studded snake bite piercings beneath her lower lip that distracted him from the prettiness of her face.

"Sorry, I just..." he started to say as a bartender guy quickly came to the girl's self imposed spotlight. She was heavily made-up and she showcased herself a low-cut top that drew the bartender's vision toward her chest.

"Can I get another Paloma...pleeeease?" she said to the bartender in a decidedly flirty voice before turning her attention back to Jim.

"So what's your story anyway, why you all like broody in the corner?" she asked, leaning against the bar and swiveling her hips. "Why don't you come have fun with us?"

Jim knew that this girl was reaching out to him, and on another night he might have seized on the opportunity, but he felt separate now. Somewhere not too far away was the one woman so different, so terrifically different from the one who was batting her eyes at him now and for her he could only feel pity and sorrow. Not for the world did he want to hurt her for her invitation, but he was not flattered by it, and he even felt a slight shame for attracting it. He yearned to be with a woman like Sam, someone in whom he had seen something that he so longed for and felt he lacked, and if Jim was articulate enough say what it was in a word he would have said, dignity, but the girl in front of him was the type that he was used to, the kind that would hang around the biker gangs in L.A., and as he glanced up at her he sensed the

55

hands of his own trailer park class clutching at him to hold him down.

"That's okay, I don't know if I'd be very good company right now," he said in an unintentionally dispirited voice.

"Oh my god, you sound like such a downer!" she said in a high-pitched squeal. She wiggled herself provocatively in front of him and he could feel the draw of her while his ego could not appreciate the adulation of her charm.

Still, all he could think of was Sam. He couldn't help but wonder what she thought of him. He was thinking of her so vividly that he was actually starting to hear the sound of her voice drowning out the noise of this girl's inebriated chattering. The voice grew clearer and he jolted to attention and back to earth. He searched the room, and sure enough, there she was.

He glanced continually at her and then noticed that every man in the room was doing the same thing. She was the type of girl who, when she walked in a place, everybody looked. He could see their heads turn, like watching a horse race. Doing nothing to draw attention to herself, a semblance of femininity projected all around her. She was dressed in a different pair of heeled leather boots, cut-off denim shorts and a white tank top. She wore smoky makeup to mask the effects of crying all evening and her brown purse dangled high and tight from her shoulder and she walked tall and moved with confidence and grace. She was with the guy that Jim had seen earlier at the Trails End Ranch, he remembered his name, Mr. Albinson.

The sight of him made Jim's heart sink and his jaw tight. He watched as she and him made their way to a back table. He felt like he wanted to hide, for despite Sam being with a man, he did not want her to see him at the bar with another girl, and for the moment he could have cursed that in him which drew women. She didn't see him, and Jim observed from a distance that Tea Cup was there and was embracing her in a hug.

Sam had a glass of red wine, while Mr. Albinson had a Jack and Diet on the rocks. They had just settled in when Tea Cup came back and rejoined them at their table.

"So Jim found ya I heard," Tea Cup said to Sam, eyeing her with curiosity.

"Yes, he did."

"Nice young man, he's here now you know."

"He is?" Sam asked with a level of enthusiasm that made her male companion take notice.

"We must get down to the matter at hand I'm afraid," Mr. Albinson said with a flip of his freshly cut and perfectly groomed golden hair.

Tea Cup ignored him and turned back to Sam. "I was sorry to hear about your father."

"Thanks," Sam said sadly yet sweetly. "I um, I have some questions for you."

"Yes, we both do," Mr. Albinson said.

"And who are you?" Tea Cup asked, squinting and frowning. Mr. Albinson was dressed in an extremely low cut, light purple v-neck shirt made of bamboo fiber that left a large portion of his clean shaven chest exposed despite his silk scarf, and although it was night, his eyes were covered by a pair of gold framed Tom Ford aviator style shades.

"Karsten," he said, before taking a sip from his icy drink through a straw.

"Yeah?" Tea Cup said as if she somehow disapproved of his very existence.

"It's okay, he's my date and he has a law degree, so we were wondering," Sam started to say before Karsten cut her off.

"Her father gave her a map."

Tea Cup tilted her head to the side. "Map did you say?"

"Yes, but we're not sure what…if it's a map to money we need to know if that money would be clean," blurted Karsten.

"Is that right," Tea Cup said in a monotone voice as she stared blank faced at Karsten.

He put his drink down. "Look, whatever, the reason we're here is because Sam has been given a map that may lead to money."

"Shhh, I wouldn't talk about stuff like that round here," Tea Cup whispered as she slid her chair
backward, looking at Karsten like she wanted to strangle him. "Come on, we can discuss this further elsewhere."

All three of them got up and walked through some back doors to a table in the darkened depths of the old Connor Hotel and Tea Cup pulled a cord from a ceiling lamp to give them light. Sam put her wine down, and took out her father's map and laid it flat on the table.

"The Lost Coast," she said as she angled it so Tea Cup could see.

"So it is," Tea Cup said as she looked with interest.

"Northern California," Sam said.

Tea Cup stroked her braid of hair and in a long drawn out way said, "Yesss…"

"Why there? Why not just send me the money instead of burying it and making it a quest like it's some forbidden treasure like a pirate?" Sam asked, leaning forward in her seat and talking with her hands in a frustrated manner.

Tea Cup smiled. "Well, old Popeye was a pirate, that's just the way he did things," she said as she reclined back in her chair. "Also, your mother didn't want him to be a part of your life, and he really didn't know where you were." She paused and held a look of amusement. "That's why he sent Jim to find you. As to why he wants you to go all the way up to California, well, maybe he just liked it up there, maybe he knows someone up there and maybe he wanted to put, whatever it is, as far away as he could from the Iron Raiders, cause if there is a large amount of cash hidden, you can bet that them boys will want it for themselves."

"But where did he get this money, Is it clean?" Karsten asked.

Tea Cup looked at him with smug disdain. "You don't know the Iron Raiders do you? Laundering money is what they do," she said. "And you two are probably too young to remember the Axis San Diego robbery."

Karsten glanced at Sam and then looked back at Tea Cup. She went on.

"Might as well tell ya. It was on a summer day in 1992, such a big deal at the time, it was all over the news. There was an explosion at a bank and three men on motorcycles were seen leaving the scene shortly after. The cops showed up and got into a high speed chase with the three guys, and they headed east on highway 8, not that you'll know where that is, but they lost em out near the mountains somewhere south of Palm Springs. The riders were able to weave off road and through the trails, go where the cops couldn't ya see," she said, speaking as if she was telling a fairy tale around a campfire. "Three motorcycles were eventually found, out in the Borrego desert, not that you'll know where that is, but there was no cash on them and no sign of the men riding them you know? The vin numbers on the bikes had all been worn off and they never could trace them back to no owners. After that it was just a big mystery, and since no one would be able to survive in the desert without transportation, it was assumed the riders were dead and the money was still somewhere out there. People went searching for it for years, still are in fact, but nobody never found a thing."

Sam sat stunned for a second until she brought her wine to her lips, drank, and then set the glass back on the table.

"How much?" Karsten asked, finally taking his sunglasses off and veering forward in his seat with eager anticipation. "How much did they steal?"

Tea Cup paused and pulled out a cigar, stuck it between her teeth and lit it by striking a match against the side of the table. "Nine million, or so they said at the time," she said, blowing smoke into the room.

Sam, turning toward Tea Cup asked, "Are you saying, that my father robbed a bank?"

"Lot of people think so," Tea Cup said. "Every year the legend grows, if I were you I'd be real careful who you trust."

"But I can't take that money," Sam said. "If that's what it is."

"Oh, that money is long since cleaned I'm sure, it doesn't really matter anymore," Tea Cup said before letting out a nostalgic sigh.

"What's this wishing tree?" Karsten asked as he studied the map.

Tea Cup shrugged and puffed on her cigar, its smoke dancing in rims of thin grey mist beneath the yellow light. Sam fidgeted in her wooden chair, causing it to creak and groan and gave Karsten a peculiar look, but said nothing.

"I don't know. I am not afraid of these Iron Raider chaps at all," Karsten said before he wrapped his mouth around his straw and sucked in his cheeks like a deflating blowfish.

Tea Cup shrugged and took a few more puffs on her cheroot. "You…will be."

While Tea Cup, Sam and Karsten were talking in the back room, Jim was still seated at the bar, sipping his third cup of joe and picking at a slice of sour-cherry pie. He felt stupid for letting himself get so enamored with Sam. Someone like her would never be interested in a guy like him, he decided, and it only made sense that a pretty girl would be with a pretty man, although the idea of that pretty man still made Jim clench his fists. He nursed his coffee and continued to listen to the live music, which was quite enjoyable compared to the ear-splitting death metal he had grown accustomed to while riding with the Raiders, but the band was quickly drowned out by seemingly his new best friend.

"Omigod look at you, you're so tan, are you Latino or something? Why won't you come drink with us?" The girl pouted as she playfully grabbed Jim's arm and shook him like he needed to be revived from a depressive stupor. He looked up into her vacant, lobotomy eyes. He didn't want to just sit around and get drunk anymore. He was better than that, he thought. He arrogantly believed that life meant more to him than it did to this girl whose thoughts did not seem to go beyond another drink and a man around her arm.

Jim had always led a secret life in his thoughts. Thoughts that he had tried to share but never found anyone capable of understanding, until he met Sam, or so he thought that he thought that she thought.

He was aware that he may have been influenced by a blinding crush, but there was something in the way Sam had looked at him, and something in the purity of her eyes made him believe that she understood him like no one else could. He drifted off again but was soon awoken by the unmistakable noise of Harleys roaring obnoxiously from the street outside.

His entire body tensed up. He looked straight ahead and told himself it was nothing to worry about. Hundreds of bikers probably passed through Jerome everyday and many of them probably frequented the Spirit Room. He spun his bar stool around to keep an eye on the entrance, only to see the bright pink face of Snod Farkus right in front of him. Snod grabbed him by the shoulder and twirled him back around so that he was once again facing the bar.

"Omigod, we were like talking," the girl said to Snod in a flabbergasted voice.

Snod growled before pushing her to the side, causing her to spill her drink and gasp in disbelief. "Two shots of Cuervo," he barked at the bartender as he leaned against the counter, claustrophobically next to Jim. "For me and this fella here," he added as he slapped Jim hard on the back.

"What do you want?" Jim asked as his mind began to race.

"You know what I want," Snod said in a threatening whisper. He was so close that Jim could smell the mix of week old food, sweat and beer on his shaggy mustache, but Jim didn't flinch.

"No, I don't," Jim said as stoically as he could.

"Why'd you run off without even sayin goodbye?"

Jim looked straight ahead and then peered out the window from the corner of his eye. He mulled over all the possible explanations as to how Snod had tracked him down, all the way to Jerome, all the way to this particular bar, but he couldn't think of any.

"What are you doing here?" he asked as the bartender returned with the two drinks.

"Nobody leaves without asking me first," Snod said before gulping down his tequila and slamming the empty shot glass on the counter.

"Okay, so I'm askin now."

"Sure you can leave," Snod said with a sardonic grunt. "But first you got to tell me where the money is!"

"What money?" Jim asked, looking down at his half eaten pie and feeling his pulse accelerating.

"Did you know that Popeye had a daughter?" Snod's haunting smile widened. He stared at Jim as if he was trying to imprint his demonic face permanently into his brain, and Jim shuttered at the thought of Snod finding out about Sam. "News to me too."

"Popeye is dead, you don't need to lurk in his shadow no more. Why don't you just move on?" Jim said as he got right in Snod's face, still seated but letting the anger explode out of him. It was then that he noticed that several other Iron Raiders had infected the Spirit Room like a virus, and he felt surrounded.

"Ain't you gonna drink, or can you not handle liquor like all you dodgasted Injuns?"

"You go ahead," Jim said after standing up and nodding at the tequila.

"Popeye never told us what he did with his cash," Snod said in an overly friendly voice like he was mocking him. "But he told you didn't he?" His smile turned to rage. He pounded his fist on the bar and took out a pistol from somewhere in his pants and pressed it into Jim's skull right above his ear. "Don't lie to me boy or I'll put a bullet through your head right here and now!"

He then pointed the gun at the ceiling and fired off two quick rounds.

Some people in the bar screamed while others ducked their heads or got all the way down on the floor. The music stopped and the room went quiet. Snod aimed the gun back at Jim.

"Where's Popeye's daughter?" He roared as he pulled out the photograph of Sam from his vest pocket while his other hand held firmly on his Sig 1911. "Tell me what I want to know!"

"I'm his daughter," a voice said from the back of the bar, shattering through the silence.

Jim froze as he watched Snod turn toward the far end of the room where Sam was standing.

"You got somethin for me doll face?" he asked with a cocky grin.

"It's not for you," Sam said with amazing stoicism.

"You got the map? Hand it over!"

"No," Sam said. Jim closed his eyes and shook his head. He knew what Snod was capable of, but Sam didn't. He noticed that as all the people had drawn their focus toward Snod and his gun, Tea Cup was slowly slinking to the other corner of the room.

"I weren't askin," Snod said as he pointed his Sig away from Jim and aimed it directly at Sam. Karsten was standing next to her and was visibly shaking and his arrogant cool demeanor had vanished completely. With a pistol now directed his way he instinctively lowered his head and spun in a panic out the back door like a chicken with its head cut off. Snod laughed out loud. "Looks like your boyfriend ain't gonna help you."

Jim knew he had to act fast. He stared at the side of Snod's face, his full attention was on Sam. He glanced at the surroundings. Boone Dix, Willie Wheeler, Meatbone, and a few other Raiders stood by and were blocking the main entrance, but their posture was lax, and they were paying more attention to Sam than anything else. Jim gritted his teeth and looked at Snod's stretched out arm that held the pistol. He burst into action and slammed Snod's wrist down with his right hand while simultaneously snatching his gun away with his left.

Snod stumbled in bewildered shock and nearly fell to the floor, while Willie Wheeler clumsily tried to pull his Glock on Jim. Just as Willie was taking aim he was blown backward by a booming shotgun blast from Tea Cup who appeared suddenly from behind the bar.

"Run!" Jim yelled at Sam as he ducked down and the shotgun fired again in the direction of frantically scattering Iron Raiders, all scrambling for their guns as well as for cover. In his peripheral, Jim saw that Sam was bolting out of the back door of the bar, and out of his sight.

Sam ran through the back hall and burst out the exit and onto the sidewalk. She looked around and tried to remember where Karsten had parked his car, and then darted to her left and around the corner to the main street. She spotted his Tesla with him already inside. The car silently moved just as she reached it and she breathlessly banged on the window to get his attention.

"Wait!" she screamed. He slammed his brakes and jolted forward and then pressed down on his brakes again and unlocked the door, allowing her to swing it open and jump inside. "What are you doing?"

"I, I'm, I don't want to die," he stammered. He kept on blinking his eyes sporadically with his hands trembling on the wheel, his face white.

"Drive!" Sam shrieked at the top of her lungs.

He rocked the car forward again and then accelerated fast and turned the vehicle toward the center of the road, only to see that he was headed straight for a mob Iron Raiders. One of them had a crowbar in his hands and Karsten had nowhere to go except straight through. He closed his eyes and sped up, but before he could impact the crowd, the pedestrian detector safety feature was alerted, and his car smoothly came to a complete stop.

The man with the crowbar then smashed in the windshield and Sam screamed. She covered her head and turned to Karsten who was now hyperventilating in the fetal position. Before the guy could swing his crowbar again, Sam opened her door, clutched her purse and stepped out of the vehicle but found herself running straight into Snod Farkus.

"Where do you think you're goin?" Snod yapped, taking a step forward. He was only inches away from Sam, who had a look of terror on her face. She madly searched through her purse and grabbed her father's envelope.

"If you want the map, you can have it, just let us go," she said, reaching out her hand, holding the envelope. He snatched it from her and smiled with bloated menace.

"Your daddy is dead little girl," he said, gripping her arm and leaning in close enough to kiss her. "Anybody ever tell you how he died?" Spit flew from his mouth as he spoke and drawing his lips to her ear he whispered, "I...killed him."

"What you want us to do with this guy Prez?" Glub Bubber, who was the guy holding the crowbar asked, looming above Karsten, just to the right of Sam and Snod.

Another shotgun blast exploded from the front of the building and instantly dispersed the crowd in all directions, pumping further chaos along the boulevard.

"Shut up and get that woman!" yelled Snod with his hand still squeezing Sam's upper arm.

"Please, don't kill me!" Sam heard Karsten scream, still in the driver's seat of his car, with Glub still hovering next to him.

Tea Cup came storming out of the Spirit Room in a mad fury as she continued to pump rounds into her Browning 12 gage and fire repeatedly. Snod ducked behind the Tesla and took Sam with him, now by pulling on her hair. He peered through the window of the car to keep an eye on Tea Cup, who was chasing the frightened horde around the corner of the building. Snod brought his back up pistol, a Ruger 9 millimeter to Sam's face.

"Your daddy's money belongs to us," he said before turning to his left to see a man on a motorcycle closing in on him fast. The rider had his right hand on the throttle while his other hand held a helmet dangling by its strap to his left. He came in quick, right at them. His speed took Snod by surprise and it caused him to freeze in place. The rider swung the helmet like a bludgeon and struck Snod square in the jaw, knocking him down hard on the pavement as well as dislodging a few of his rotten teeth. The rider stopped. It was Jim.

"Get on," he said to Sam after dropping the helmet and kicking the bike into neutral. She sat on the ground stupefied, looking down the road where she could hear and see Karsten running away from Glub Bubber, screaming.

Snod wiped the blood from his face and shook his head like a wet dog as he attempted to get his bearings. He saw his gun laying on the ground in front of him and picked it up.

Sam looked at Jim and without hesitating a second longer, hopped onto the back of his bike, shoved her purse between her thighs and instinctively wrapped her arms around his torso. Jim slammed into gear and took off with a burst, narrowly missing running over Snod's legs as he rolled over on the ground and out of the way in the nick of time.

"Hold on tight!" Jim yelled as loud as he could while he accelerated into third and then forth gear and leaned into a hairpin turn. They continued to speed up, blasting out of the curve like a slingshot and blazing down the hill into the valley. Jim could hear and almost feel the bullets flying past them as they rode away, but he kept his eyes deeply focused on what was ahead, clunked into 5th gear and didn't look back.

Once they were safely out of sight, and back into the calm of the desert night at the bottom of the hill, Jim took a right onto 89A in Clarkdale, just a mile or two down the road, and headed east toward Cottonwood. From there he decided to get off the main highway, just to lose anyone who may have been trying to follow them. He saw a sign that said Dead Horse Ranch and he felt Sam hitting him in the shoulder.

"Stop!" she yelled. He slowed down and pulled into a deserted parking lot and killed the engine.

"What?" he asked as he pushed the kickstand down and stepped off the bike.

"Just, we need to stop!" Sam said frantically before getting off herself. "What is going on?"

Jim paced around and ran his hands through his hair.

"I don't know," he said before walking right up to her and looking straight into her panicked eyes. "I'm sorry."

"They tried to kill us, they almost did!"

"I know, I don't know how they…" He trailed off and put his head down.

"Did you lead them to me or something?" she shrieked as she pushed him away.

"No, I didn't! Why would I do that?" he said, as he patrolled the dark parking lot and kept his eyes peeled for any unwanted visitors. "Come on, we need to go."

"What's at the end of that map, nine million?"

Jim stopped and answered honestly. "I really don't know."

She bent her knees and looked down at the asphalt. Her face had gone pale and she was breathing heavily. "Just, take me home."

Jim tilted his head and exhaled. "I wouldn't go home, may not be safe there."

"Why? They got what they wanted," she said. "I gave them the map!"

"They don't leave loose ends."

She stared at him blank faced, like she couldn't believe what was happening. "Should we call 911?"

"What would we tell them?"

Sam considered his question for a moment and then said, "Fine, I'll just walk!"

He could see in her eyes that he wasn't going to talk her out of anything. She walked away from him, out of the parking lot and toward the street. He ran after her.

"Wait," he said. She stopped and turned his way. "Come on, I'll take you home."

She stood still for a moment, but then turned around and they got back on the motorcycle together and meandered through the backstreets of Cottonwood until they returned to route 89A. Sam directed him toward her apartment in West Sedona from the back of the bike. It was a rundown little complex of early 1980's construction on the edge of town but it was apparent from the moment they arrived, that something was amiss, although Sam wasn't sure why.

She got off first and noticed from a distance that the light was on in the window of her studio. She stared perplexed and went closer before Jim stopped her.

"What is it?" he asked in a cautious whisper.

"I don't know but I'm gonna find out," she said, giving him a fearful glance before lurching away and heading for the stairs on the outside of the building.

Jim surveyed the surroundings. Everything was quiet and calm and Sedona's Dark-Sky community ordinance made the night beyond the parking lot pitch black. He shook his head in disbelief of the situation he found himself in, before he followed her up the stairs.

When he reached the second floor he saw that, aside from her breathing, Sam was standing still, like she was frozen in the entrance to her apartment, with the door cracked open. He came up right beside her. They looked at each other and paused, before Jim pushed the door open.

The apartment was a mess. Books and bedding and clothes were scattered all over the floor, chairs were toppled over and dresser drawers were ajar, but more concerning than all that was the smell. The entire apartment reeked strongly of gasoline, and it was obvious to Jim that the Iron Raiders had found out where Sam lived and had been looking for the map, before, or perhaps during the time that Snod had tracked her down in Jerome.

Sam looked around, her face in shock, and Jim led her back to the outside corridor. She took a deep breath of the warm night air and placed her hands on her knees. He knelt in front of her.

"Do you have any valuables in there?"

She didn't answer.

"You got a cat?"

She shook her head.

"I'm so sorry, I should've known better," he said, trying to sound as comforting as possible. "This is all my fault."

She let out a sudden and sharp gasp like she had been drowning in the ocean and had just reached the surface. "What's wrong with these people?"

He stood up and peered over the flimsy metal banister, still very aware that whoever tore up Sam's apartment could still be close by. He turned back and placed his hands on her shoulders and looked her in the eye. "It's not safe to be here."

"I don't, I don't umm," she stammered. "I don't get it, they have the envelope, why would they do this?"

Jim paused and tilted his head in deep speculation. "Do you have anyplace you can go or anyone you can call?"

She thought of the handful of men that she knew would happily share their bed if she asked. She thought of some of her girlfriends that lived nearby but her mind was still racing with anxiety. She didn't think she'd be able to sleep for a second until she knew for sure she was safe, and she didn't much feel like seeing anyone. All she could think about was the look on that man's face, telling her smugly that he was the one who killed her father.

She thought again about calling the police. She wondered why Jim hadn't called them already. She was so scared and angry that she felt numb, and it showed in her blank expression. Then an awful smell of smoke and burning rubber caught her attention.

"Come on," Jim said as he took her by the hand and gently guided her back to the stairs. They peered over the railing down into the parking lot and saw that Sam's red Honda was on fire. She gasped and followed him almost blindly down the steps, but as they rounded the corner, halfway down, she looked up and saw two men wearing black leather vests and cut-off sleeves. She grabbed Jim's hand a little tighter and stopped.

Both men had their hands full with fast-food bags from Vortex Burger and drinks with straws. Jim recognized the one on the right to be Flash Fontana but he did not recognize the other guy. They all stared at each other in silence for a long moment, with the two men on street level and Jim and Sam still several steps up.

Flash dropped his drink and food on the ground and ripped out a revolver from inside his cut. Jim sprang to attention and grasped the rails on either side of him with both hands and lifted his body off the ground. He used gravity to gain momentum and swung his legs down toward Flash and kicked him solidly in the face with his rubber soled cowboy boots. Flash was immediately knocked back so hard and so fast that his head slammed into the building behind him and his gun flew from his grip. Jim released from the railings and landed flat on his feet at the bottom of the stairs.

Sam boldly ran down the concrete steps and instinctively picked up Flash's gun from the ground while the other guy bull-rushed Jim and pinned him against the wall next to the stairs. The guy had his hands around Jim's neck and he dug his thumbs into his suprasternal notch and pressed down. Jim gasped for air and attempted to knee the guy in the stomach and groin but he was unable to put enough force into it to get him off. The guy then put Jim in a headlock and spun him around. Sam looked up at him and pulled back the hammer of the revolver and aimed. Her legs and fingers felt reduced to putty, afraid to fire because they were moving so sporadically. She took a deep breath and went straight up to the guy as he strangled Jim and pressed the barrel of the gun right into his thigh and pulled the trigger.

The shot went off and the man screamed in a spasm of extreme pain and Jim grabbed him by the head and neck and brutally shoved his face into the metal railing causing the guy's body to go limp and collapse onto the concrete. Jim turned to Sam.

"We need to go now!"

She stood at the bottom of the stairs, shaking. Jim had to pry the 38 special from her fingers and he stuffed it under the waistband of his jeans behind him and took her by the hand and led her around the disabled bodies that lay on the ground. They ran past her flaming car, back to his bike together, and peeled out of there like a wild mustang frightened by a coyote, but not before hearing the deafening sound of the car exploding in a huge burst of flames behind them.

Jim rode without a plan and without thinking where he was going. He headed north toward downtown Sedona, keeping his speed reasonable so as to not draw any attention from Police, but all the while envisioning Flash getting up off the ground and hopping on his beast of a machine and chasing them down. Flash had received his nickname for a reason. He rode a muscled up V-Rod that Jim was certain could outrun his Scout if put to the test.

Jim navigated through roundabouts as they got deeper into town and kept a close watch on his rearview mirrors. He could swear he could see a motorcycle following them and he continued going straight, right into Oak Creek Canyon, and as all signs of civilization disappeared, he picked up his speed on the narrow two lane road that was winding up the side of a mountain toward Flagstaff, hoping to lose his tail.

Sam sat behind him and wrapped her arms as tight as she could around his waist. When she looked down at the small of his back she was confronted by the revolver that was still stuffed in the waistband of his pants and shining in the moonlight. She knew she ought to feel sick to her stomach, but, she didn't. Instead she felt a natural high of adrenaline pulsing through her body and the intuition of survival overtaking her fear. Wearing no helmet, she felt simultaneously free and helpless, much like her hair blowing wildly against the backdrop of the diamond studded sky. There was nothing she could do but hold on and watch the black trees fly by like shadows, and hope that the man in front of her knew what he was doing.

*"I slipped on her shoe, she was a perfect size seven."*

Sam woke up sometime in the dark of the early morning in a panic. She wasn't in her own bed and she had no recollection of where she was or how she got there. There was no one in the bed but her, and she looked around the room frantically as her eyes adjusted to the blackness.

Above was a ceiling of exposed wooden logs and the walls were the same. She sat up. There was a man lying on the floor, hardly visible. She began to remember. It was Jim, fully dressed with only a pillow beneath his head and he was asleep. She laid back down as her heart rate slowed. The image and smell of her apartment flashed in her mind and haunted her and her car exploding, and shooting that guy made her shutter. The memory of Karsten and the man with the crowbar preyed upon her, and it settled in, that this blur of events, her father, the map, and the guns, was not a nightmare but were things that actually happened. She closed her eyes and utter exhaustion battled back and forth with horror for what seemed like hours, until she passed out.

When she awoke again she was flooded with bright sunlight beaming through the windows, and after blinking and rubbing her eyes with her fingers she realized that the room was now empty. There was a plastic bottle of water on the nightstand, and she opened it and drank like her life depended on it. Tossing the sheets and blankets to the side she stumbled toward the bathroom mirror to the left of the queen-sized bed. Still in her cut-off jean shorts and camisole, her hair was a tangled brown mess. She ran water through her hands and splashed it over the smudged makeup on her face before putting on and lacing up her stylish brown boots, grabbing the water and heading outside.

The light blinded her again and it took her a second to get a grasp of her surroundings. There was a complex of dozens of tiny log cabins with the long and imposing red Vermilion cliffs in the not too distant background and a cloudless blue sky above. In front of her cabin was the black Indian Scout and next to it was Jim. He was kneeling, and deeply focused on the bike, investigating it so close that he didn't notice her.

"What are you doing?" she asked.

He spun around, startled, still in his crouched position.

"I uh, I still can't figure how they found me."

She looked at him and sat down on the wooden front steps of the cabin. "Maybe they just found me."

He stared at her and ran his hand through his messy black hair. "How?"

She thought about it for a moment but couldn't think of an answer. She fidgeted with her french tipped nails while continuing to look around, still waking up. "Where are we?"

"Utah, a town called Kanab."

"Utah?" she asked, bewildered. It was so dark and she had been so tired the previous night, that she didn't remember crossing any state lines. She remembered that they had stopped at a gas station somewhere off highway 89. She recalled snippets of their conversations, Jim giving her his jacket to wear and telling her that they needed to get as far away from Sedona as possible, but after that it was a blur of darkness.

"Remember, we almost stopped in Page, but it just seemed too obvious so we kept goin, should be safe now," he said, squinting through the bright light of the morning sun to the east. "You were pretty out of it, didn't get in till after one in the morning, towards the end I got worried you was goin to fall asleep and fall off the bike."

He shot her a crooked smile, but she didn't smile back. He sighed. "Look, I'm so sorry for all this." He spoke with sadness in his voice. "I can take you wherever you want to go, if you wanna go to the police, I get it."

Her eyes came up from the asphalt parking lot and fixated on his. "Whatever my dad buried out there, they sure seem to want it bad."

"They'll do anything for money," he said before standing up and looking at his bike. She hoisted herself to her feet as well and went toward him.

"I might have killed that man," she said as her eyes went wide.

"You saved my life."

"You don't think I did kill him, do you?"

"He'll live."

"Will the police be…"

"No," he said, looking straight at her. "It was their gun, and we have it…and Iron Raiders never talk to cops."

She exhaled a slight sigh of relief and then looked at him with a turn of disgust as she felt all the anger and frustration in her life coming to a boil. "I was doing fine before I met you."

"I'm sorry," he said in a nervous whisper.

"You're sorry? I don't have a home anymore, I don't have a car, I was almost killed and all you can say is, ``I'm sorry?''

They stared at each other for a long moment before Jim shook his head and took a step back.

"You're right, if it weren't for me none of this woulda happened, I brought all this to you, I was just tryin to honor your father's wishes."

"You guys were both idiots!" she said, throwing her hands in the air. "Clueless!"

"I'm-"

"Don't say you're sorry again!" she yelled. She turned away and pressed her hands against her temples. "Why did you take me all the way out here again?"

"I just wanted to get you somewhere safe, somewhere they wouldn't find you. I didn't know what to do, I don't know how they found you or how they found me, I just knew we had to get far away!"

"I was safe before I met you!" she said, looking straight at him. "And now we're stuck in the middle of nowhere, that was your plan? Do you even have a plan?"

He took another step back and looked down. "My plan was to keep you safe, that was all I thought about." He sighed, put his hands in his pockets and tensed his shoulders. "I'll take you somewhere else, to a friend or family or wherever."

"I don't have any family anymore," she said as her voice intensified again. "My dad was the last one, now it's just me."

"I ain't have no…any family neither," he said as he looked down again and paused. "Where do you want me to take you?"

He peered back into her eyes and saw that the expression on her face had grown more deliberate as her anger subsided. She had made her point, and she wanted him to hear it, but her true state of mind was elsewhere. She pursed her lips and gazed at him, her brain flooded with a multitude of emotions as she was reminded of the previous night's feeling of exhilaration while the desperate yearn to attack the world full throttle pulled at the strings of her heart and fought with her repugnance. The mysterious desires of facing all life's spirit-groping and soul reaching head on infiltrated her, and the sight of Jim suddenly sent her pulse thrilling with severe thoughts and feelings for reasons she could not explain.

"I don't really have a lot of money," she said.

"Before your Dad died, he gave me cash," he said, a little confused by the swing of her mood and attitude. "He gave it to me I guess cause he wanted me to have something, and he wanted me to find you."

She became silent and ran her fingers through her long soft hair. "I'm hungry," she said finally. "You took me all the way out here, the least you can do is buy me breakfast."

"Yeah, okay."

She reached her hand out toward him. "You have a little, um, blood on your shirt."

He lowered his head and saw the reddish brown stain near his shoulder. Splatter resulting from Tea Cup's shotgun blasts. "Yeah, I should, uh, change it, and get cleaned up."

"I would like to take a shower too."

She closed her eyes and then opened them, looking right at him. "And then after breakfast you are going to take me to the Lost Coast."

Jim's eyes bulged round, amazed by her words and the way she was dealing with the recent events. She had a look of extreme determination burning out of her.

"You serious?"

"Yes, I am," she said, this time even more deliberate. "This thing will get us there right?"

She gave the front motorcycle tire a little kick.

"That's a, that's a…I don't know if that's a good idea," he stammered as he scratched his head and tugged on his hair.

There was a long moment of silence.

"This is Kanab you said?"

"Yeah."

She tilted her head over to the main road on her left, deep in thought. "You know, this is supposed to be the place where the great treasure of Montezuma is buried, in Kanab."

"What's…Montezuma?"

"He was an Aztec king."

He stared at her, trying to figure out what she was trying to say, and not wanting to sound stupid or risk getting yelled at again. "Buried treasure huh?"

"Yep," she said, nodding as her face softened.

"Where'd you learn that?"

"In school."

His eyes lowered back to the pavement, sheepish and embarrassed. "I ain't never really went to school."

Her lips closed together, she found herself feeling sympathy and something fierce for him although not knowing why. It was as if she was so overwhelmed that she needed lighthearted conservation just to cope. "What did you do, I mean like did you do something for a living, back in L.A.?"

"A few things," he said, surprised by her efforts to get to know him in that moment so soon after such a traumatic experience. "Actually worked some straight jobs, unlike most of the guys."

"Like what?"

"Landscape work, electric arc welding."

"Why welding?"

He shrugged. "Don't know." He looked down while still maintaining eye contact. "Guess since I grew up with everything around me being broken, I wanted to learn how to fuse things back together permanently, so they would never part again."

His voice had become slow and heavy with emotion.

"Did you like it?"

He stared off in the distance while a small grin formed on his lips. "Well, it's not riveting," he said as his smirk broke into a dimpled grin.

Still slightly angry at him, she tried not to smile.

"That was a...that was a little joke," he said.

Rolling her eyes she took a step forward, her feet only inches from his, his boots so big and clunky in comparison to her own. "This is not your fault. If I need someone to blame I should blame my father, not you. Whatever is over there," she said before pausing and peering out across the vast desert horizon where Utah met Arizona. "My dad wanted me to have it, and they killed him. I don't want to just sit back and let them take it."

There was fire and conviction in her voice, but Jim knew the Iron Raiders well, and she didn't. "They have the map, and it's just too dangerous," he said.

She knew from the moment the words 'too dangerous' left his tongue that they were not normally part of his limited vocabulary. She found herself absorbed in trying to reconcile his words of caution and carefulness with the intensity she saw in his face. His eyes expressed so much potential and power that they made her believe he could do anything he set his mind to. Despite her anger she found that her eyes could not stop drawing themselves to his shoulders and there was a sweetness in the thought of laying her hands on them and resting her head against them as she had done from the back of the motorcycle the night before. She reached into the back pocket of her shorts and took out her phone.

"They may have the map, but so do we," she said as she slowly pressed her shoulder into his side so he would have a clear view of her screen. He felt sparks flying throughout his body as her touch seemed to heighten all of his other senses while simultaneously dulling his powers of thought. He saw that the map Popeye had sent her was now on the screen of her phone as clear as the sheet of paper itself. The idea that she had such foresight to take a picture made him smile. She looked up into his eyes, still standing next to the motorcycle as the sun highlighted her hair. "I don't think we have any choice. So…let's get going."

Glub Bubber and Billy Coxwain entered a musty room at the Iron Horse Motel in Flagstaff, Arizona. Flash Fontana staggered in behind them. It had been complete madness the night before, as the huge mob of Iron Raiders had to hightail it out of Jerome before the cops showed up. Willie Wheeler was dead, but the rest of them headed north and crashed at the dingy inn that the club had used several times in the past. Snod Farkus sat on the bed and looked at Flash.

"Tumbleweed did that to you?" he asked as he pressed his dirty fingers into his mouth, investigating his broken teeth.

"He sucker punched me," Flash said.

"Sucker punched you in the face?"

Flash stared at Snod's own battered mug, knowing full well that Tumbleweed had gotten him too, but he said nothing.

"The girl was there?" Snod asked.

"Yeah," Flash said. "She shot Vince Ferragamo!"

"And you let em get away! You spineless blockhead," Snod said before going back to staring at the map that was unfolded next to him on the mattress. "What the hully gee is a wishin tree?" he asked in a general way as he scratched his long slick hair.

"Wish I knew," Glub said with a smirk. Snod glared at him and Glub nervously cleared his throat and quickly turned his face more serious.

"That some kinda inside thing between him and his daughter?" Snod asked the room and then stared hard at Billy. "Popeye writin in code? How about it?"

"How should I know," Billy said in a deep voice as he raised his hands in the air and then walked to the dresser drawers and grabbed himself a warm beer.

"Ya'll a bunch of worthless bilge sucking lubbers," Snod yelled as he stood up and glared back at Flash. "Vince Ferragamo looks worse than you," he added before turning to Boone Dix. "Tumbleweed still in Utah?"

"Yep," Boone said as he stood with his cell phone in hand.

"Why'd he go there?" Snod asked. "He still with the girl?"

"This just shows me where the tracker is located," Boone said with an amused look on his face.

"It don't have no video option?" Snod asked in all seriousness.

"It don't work like that," Boone said, blank faced.

"I told ya they rode off together, I saw them!" Flash said.

"Well no more waistin time," Snod said. "Billy, you and Boone need to leave now, and take Flash with you so he can remedy his screw up, but remember, no one kills Tumbleweed but me."

"What are you gonna do?" Boone asked.

"Time to round up the troops, we're goin... on a treasure hunt!"

90

Jim and Sam sat across from each other at a booth in the Kanab Creek Diner. The place was busier than it looked from the outside, and its dark wooden interior gave it a warm and friendly atmosphere. They were hungry, and both in need of coffee. Jim had a stack of buttery pancakes in front of him and Sam was working on strawberry and whipped cream Belgian waffles.

"What?" Sam asked after she finished chewing, as she noticed Jim looking at her inquisitively.

"What about your job?" he asked as he brought hot coffee to his lips.

She put her fork down, and said, "I quit."

Jim placed his mug on the table and looked back at her, struggling for words. They both became quiet for a few moments, making the surrounding noises of dishes clanging, coffee cups being filled, people talking, and Neil Young singing through the overhead speakers, more noticeable. "And what about that guy you were with?"

Sam nearly laughed out loud and then frowned. "He turned out to be quite something," she said as she adjusted herself in her seat, somewhat ashamed. She paused. "He owns a few horses, he's been trying to ask me out for months and last night I finally said yes." She shrugged. "I was lonely and sad and I thought he might be able to help me, it was a mistake. I really don't know him that well."

Jim stayed mute for several seconds before taking a bite of his pancakes. "Yeah, okay," he said with his mouth full.

She ate more strawberries and cream off the top of her waffle and then stopped. "Where did you learn to fight like that?" she asked before placing the fork between her lips again.

He leaned back in his seat and finished chewing. "Your father, he taught me to defend myself, but really I don't know how to fight. It's just when I seen you in danger I just uh…" He trailed off and placed more pancakes in his mouth, feeling awkward. He chewed and tried to think of something else to say. All he could come up with was, "It's a long way to the ocean."

"Yeah."

"Have you traveled much?"

"Not since I was a kid," she said. "It's been a few years since I've been out of the state actually."

"Why's that?"

"Work, and never could afford to go anywhere really. My mom got sick right when I was about to graduate from high school, and uh, her family lost a bunch of money during the recession so we didn't have the best insurance and…um…"

"I'm sorry," Jim said, hearing the sorrow in her voice. "What was she like?"

"My mom? She was…I guess you could say that my father married up."

She spoke with a coy smile that Jim decided was most adorable.

"What was...he like?" she asked. "My dad...before he died."

Jim put his fork on his plate. "He was good, he um, lost a few teeth, but he quit drinkin a few years back, I think he cleaned up a lot."

She finished chewing and licked a small dab of whipped cream off her lower lip. "I wish I would have seen him, had a relationship with him, before he died."

"Why...didn't you?"

"I was 18, I was angry," she said after a deep sigh. "All I ever heard from my mom was, what a terrible guy he was. She cut off all contact. I just wish I would have made an effort, so that I could make up my own mind about him. But it's too late now."

She stared at him for a moment, then took another bite of her waffles as if to distract herself and prevent more than the single tear that was running down her cheek.

She wiped her face with a clean paper napkin and there was a long pause.

"You sure about this?" he asked.

"No, but I have nowhere else to go."

"It's dangerous."

She saw that he was now smiling through his eyes. "Riding a motorcycle is dangerous," she said.

"Maybe we should get you a dome, you should probably get some longer pants too."

"I would really like a toothbrush."

"Are you scared?" he asked in a more serious tone.

"Yeah, but mostly just..."

As she started to say the words out loud, the reality of her situation hit her with sobering brutality. "I'm leaving everything, I don't even really have a home anymore, I'm homeless."

"Me too," he said.

They talked a while longer and ate until both of their plates were clean. They then hopped back on the bike and slowly circled around town until they spotted a little thrift store.

"I guess I'll see what they have," she said after stepping off the motorcycle in front of the shop.

"Don't be too picky, just get somethin to protect your legs," he said, still seated on the bike. "But we need to get movin soon."

"Easy for a man to say."

She gave him a look and he rode over to the other side of the street. He filled the bike with mid-grade fuel, bought a toothbrush and sunscreen, as was her request, and stocked up on bottled water at a Chevron station. He then went back to the consignment store to pick her up. He parked and waited, and she walked out several minutes later.

She was in the same white tank top as before, but she now had her hair tied back in a brown bandana, her eyes concealed in dark oval sunglasses and her legs poured into light blue distressed jeans with holes above the knees exposing her skin.

"Well?" she asked as she held her arms out at her sides. "All changed and ready to go."

Jim was stunned, and he could feel his heart rate accelerating. "Yeah, you look like you're ready for a motorcycle trip," he said as nonchalantly as he could while he leaned against the bike and tried his best to look cool.

"Maybe a little snug, but there weren't really a whole lot of options," she said, tugging on the waistband. She gazed at him in just his tight white t-shirt, Levi's and shades with the sunshine bouncing off his hair and she thought he looked quite handsome. "Don't we need jackets?"

"Nah, it's too hot, I stuffed mine in the saddlebag. You can wear it if you want, but, I won't crash...I promise."

"We do need to get helmets though."

"I told ya I won't crash," he said with a smile. "No dome law in Utah, but we'll have to buy some down the road at some point."

"Am I supposed to lean a certain way when you turn or anything?" she asked as she placed her hands on the rear-seat backrest and drew her eyes to his.

Jim had been on motorcycles since he was 10, but the times that he had actually ridden with another person on the back were few and far between, despite his Indian Scout being equipped with a substantial passenger seat.

Riding with Sam did feel different, and it was an adjustment. Quite literally an adjustment, as Jim had already tightened up the suspension sag that morning while she was in the shower to accommodate the extra weight.

"Just do what you did last night and, don't fall off," he said with a smirk as he wrapped his legs around the engine. "And don't tickle me. If you tickle me, we both die."

"I can't believe I'm doing this."

He fired it up and she got on behind him and cinched up her bandana good and tight before they took off.

They went north, continuing on route 89 toward Mt. Carmel Junction. It was a beautiful day, temperatures in the upper 80's and steadily climbing with the sun. The road had no shortage of breathtaking scenery of red rock cliffs, forested mountains and twisting gorges. Sam took in the sweet smells of the junipers, pinyons, and ponderosa pines as they split through the southwest's grand circle between Zion and Bryce Canyon. Weekend riders passed frequently going the opposite direction and they all waved at them and Sam waved back. The breeze was warm and soft all the way through and the two-lane highway followed a crystal clear alpine stream to the town of Orderville, all the way to the highway 14 intersection. From there they turned west.

Billy Coxwain drove a white Ford cargo van north at 70 miles per hour on highway 89A. Boone Dix sat to his right and Flash Fontana laid sprawled out in the seat behind them. They had just passed the town of Cameron, Arizona, a good 50 miles or so out of Flagstaff.

"Ever been to the Grand Canyon?" Boone asked Billy.

"Nope," Billy said blankly in his distinctive deep voice.

"Ever wanted to?" Boone asked.

"Nope."

"How can you say that?"

"It's just a big hole in the ground." Billy said.

Boone looked over at him. Billy, who was from the North Phoenix chapter, didn't talk much, but he had a habit of leaving his mouth open after he was finished speaking, and it was starting to drive Boone nuts.

"You don't know that if you've never been!" Boone said.

Billy stayed silent for several seconds with his hands on the wheel and his eyes straight ahead. "You been?"

"Yeah."

"So it ain't a big hole in the ground?"

Boone clenched his jaw and went back to looking at his cell phone and then said, "What's the plan when we find em?"

"I can think of a few things," Flash said from the backseat.

"He said he wants em alive," Boone said.

"Did you know Popeye had a daughter?" Flash asked in a whimsical voice.

"No," Boone said.

"Not bad to look at neither," Flash said as he sat up straight and leaned toward Boone. "Whooo-eee...not bad at all."

"Don't get any ideas," Boone said with a turn of his head. "She probably ain't even wit Tumbleweed no more."

"Where is he now?" Billy asked.

"North of Zion," Boone said as he looked back at his phone. "You ever been to Zion?"

"Nope," Billy said.

Sam and Jim stopped off at a motorcycle dealership in Cedar City and bought a couple of open faced half-helmets for around forty dollars each. Not wanting to waste time, they pressed on into Nevada and turned right at the small Mormon town of Panaca, and headed north on highway 93. They got to know each other quickly, as they were forced into very close proximity, and each new sight and old west themed motel conjured up romantic dreams in Jim's head.

After about a hundred miles of grueling high desert with nothing but sage brush dotting the landscape, they went west onto highway 50 until they reached the town of Ely, which was located exactly in the middle of nowhere. The last hour or so had been particularly brutal, as the heat exceeded body temperature, making it extremely difficult to cool down, and they were both desperate for refuge.

"This okay?" Jim asked after pulling over at the first, and possibly only restaurant around, a grimy hole in the side of a brick building with the name 'Slimy Joe's', on the front.

"I don't care, I just need a break," Sam said in a breathy voice, speaking over the patter of the motor, as she placed her hands on Jim's shoulders from her seated position behind him. "It's not like there's a whole lot of options."

"Right," he said as he backed into a parking spot and killed the engine. He got off the bike first and took in the area. Ely was a former silver mining town, but it was situated in a valley surrounded by steep mountains, seemingly on all sides. It felt from another time, even the vehicles parked on the sides of the road were outdated, and Jim had to search around for a while before he spotted a car that was made after 1990.

Despite the blistering heat and sun beating down on them, the town looked bleak and cold. It struck Jim that everything in Nevada appeared to have a grey hue to it, in comparison to the golden yellows of Utah. As they walked to the door together, Jim noticed a motorcycle parked at the side of the entrance. An old low ride Harley Ironhead 900 with black riveted saddlebags on each side.

They went into the restaurant and collapsed into a booth in the corner. The place looked sketchier than Jim had initially thought. There were no windows, and the room was dimly lit with fluorescent overhead lights that hummed louder than the Merle Haggard music playing in the background. There were slot machines decorating the wall and a woman in a black leather cut was utilizing one of them. There was a mix of old and young men slumped together, up front at the bar, all of which had turned and stared at them when they entered, some staring a little longer at Sam.

Jim made eye contact with the lone bartender, perhaps Slimy Joe himself, but received only a glare back, as if the guy resented new customers.

"You sure this place is okay?" Jim asked Sam as he shifted his eyes around the room.

"I don't care. It has air-conditioning and a place to charge my phone," she said as she slid her bandana off, let her hair down and fanned herself with her hand. Her normally milky olive skin was already a shade or two darker from constant exposure.

They waited for a while longer, with Sam resting her arms on the table like she was ready to fall asleep, her mind questioning whether or not this whole plan wasn't a terrible idea.

"What do you want to eat?" Jim finally asked. He had expected someone to come serve them, but after several minutes and evaluating the place again, that seemed doubtful.

"I'll eat anything at this point," she said.

"Burger and fries okay?"

She adjusted her posture. "Yes, and a... maybe a coke or a Pepsi or something."

He nodded, got up and walked to the bartender, a more than middle aged man with a thin comb over, poorly masking his balding head.

"Can we order some food?"

"Menus on the wall," said the bartender with a shrug, acting like it wasn't his job to help anybody figure out how to order. There was a younger white guy with a draft beer and an empty shot glass in front of him, and he audibly snickered as he turned and watched Jim glance toward the menu. He was a big guy, muscular through the shoulders and neck with a navy blue Dallas Cowboys hat on. A short, neatly groomed chinstrap beard framed the lower half of his oval face. He had a certain look about him that said he belonged in prison.

"I just want two cheeseburgers and fries and a couple of waters and uh, maybe some coffee if you got any," Jim said, turning back to the bartender. "Oh, and a large coke."

"We'll bring it out," the bartender said, annoyed.

Jim went back and wearily sat down and Sam excused herself to find the restroom. The snickering Dallas Cowboys guy at the bar, very obviously had his eyes fixated on her and every move she made, to the point where he may as well have been drooling out of the side of his mouth. He gawked even harder when she came back, the two inch heels of her boots clicking in haughty cadence, giving the bar an unfamiliar womanly aura as she sat back down across from Jim.

Several minutes later, the bartender arrived at their table with two hearty burgers dripping with cheese, as well as fries, waters, coke and even the coffee, much to Jim's surprise. He grabbed some ketchup and they dug into their food with vigor, both hungrier than they thought.

"Oh wow," Sam said after she finished chewing. "I didn't know I could work up such an appetite from just sitting on the back of a bike."

"Hours in the desert will do that to you," Jim said before sinking his teeth back into his half eaten burger.

"How far do you want to go today?" she asked, peeking at her phone, which she had plugged into the outlet on the wall to her right.

"As far as we can I guess."

"I never realized just how far away everything is. Do you think we can beat them there?"

"Maybe."

"We have an advantage though."

"How do you mean?"

"How carefully did you look at the map?" she asked, zooming in on the phone's screen with her fingers. "The wishing tree, it's not a specific location, they're not going to know what that is."

Jim took sip of his coffee and eyed her curiously. "And you do?"

"Yes," she said, raising her eyebrows. "One of the last times I was with my dad, I was there."

"You've been to this wishing thing before?"

"Mm-hmm," she said. "Before my mom totally cut ties with him. I used to tell him it was my favorite place in the world. There was this amazing tree there, my dad told me that if I wrote down a wish on a piece of paper and buried it next to that tree, someday it would come true."

Her gaze became unfocused and she bit her lower lip as if she had become lost in some sort of amusement.

"You saying that you've been to the exact location on the map?"

She sighed, and with her elbow on the table, rested her chin in her palm. Her eyes darted back at him. "The wishing tree was a special place for my dad and I, maybe the only thing we had together."

He leaned in closer. "What did you wish for?"

Pushing herself forward she brushed a wisp of hair away from her eye and gazed at him dreamily. "Get me there safe and I'll tell you."

"I uh," he stammered, drawing his head back and pausing. "You know I weren't expecting none of this. I was just gonna keep my promise to

Popeye, get the envelope to you, and then, just uh…"

"And do what?"

"Don't know, disappear some place, explore the West on my own for once, start a new life."

"Starting a new life sounds nice," she said as she unconsciously grazed on the remaining fries, having already finished her burger. "I wasn't expecting this either, but um, I'm glad I'm doing this with you and not by myself, and not with Karsten."

She smiled between bites and he heard his heart beating louder in his chest. "You staying comfortable enough back there?"

"Uhhh…no…the seat's too small, my butt is killing me," she said as she nonchalantly dipped another fry into the tiny paper cup of ketchup. As she was chewing her eyes perked up. "But the views have been amazing."

He tried to think of something he could do or say to make her feel more at ease, but all he came up with was, "You see a lot more than you do in a car."

"Totally," she said with a hint of excitement before her face turned melancholy again. "Feel a lot more too."

They sat for a minute in silence, both of them eyeing the other and then awkwardly turning away as if they were fearful of holding each other's gaze for too long.

"It's such a shame really," she said, floating away. "My dad could have had such an amazing life if he didn't screw around and just stayed with my mom. He'd still be alive, who knows maybe she would be too."

They both became quiet again.

"We should probably get going," Jim said finally.

"Yeah, where is this guy?" She looked impatiently at the bartender and slid out of the booth. "Hold on."

"Here," he said as handed her some cash and got up himself. "I'll throw this stuff away and use the restroom one more time."

He tossed their trash in a can in the back and then headed to the bathroom while Sam went in the opposite direction toward the bar.

"Can we get the check please?" she asked, feeling like she had to fight to get the bartender to do anything. She stood, almost on her tippy toes right behind some of the slumped over barflies in an attempt to peer over them without getting too close. The guy with the Dallas Cowboy cap turned to his left and feasted on Sam's alluring figure, drawing his eyes unabashedly to her waist, her breasts, and then to her bare shoulder which was only partially hidden by her long brown hair. He then zeroed his focus on her backside and exhaled deeply.

"Why you in such a rush to leave?" he asked with a lustful, dead-eyed stare. "What's a girl like you doin in a place like this anyway?"

His words frightened her. They were not coming out of friendly curiosity.

"I'm with someone," she said plainly and coldly. Now her own words surprised her, speaking of Jim as if he was her boyfriend.

"I don't see nobody," the guy said, as he spun his whole body toward her while staying firmly planted on the barstool. "If you get tired of that motorcycle I got a nice big comfy truck for you, I'd take ya wherever you want to go."

"I'm kind of in a hurry and I just want the check," she said in a louder voice, causing the bartender to finally acknowledge.

Much to her horror, the Dallas Cowboys guy rose to his feet and took a step or two closer.

"Why don't you stay a while, let me buy you a drink," he said before reaching out his thick stubby hand and grabbing her wrist.

"Don't touch me!" she said, pulling herself away.

"Leave her alone," said a voice from the opposite side of the room. Sam turned and saw that it was the woman that had been glued to the slot machines. She was middle-aged and her face was tan and dark. Her black hair was intricately woven beneath a bandana into long braids that went well down her back, and a single gold earring held high to her earlobe. She was a small woman, but she didn't seem the least bit intimidated.

"What are you gonna do about it?" the Dallas Cowboys guy said in a smug voice as he turned his hips at the woman and put his hand on a gun that was holstered to his waist. Sam was astonished by how many people seemed to be packing heat lately. Everyone seated at the bar had their attention on the confrontation that was taking place now, but they all turned when the door to the restroom opened and Jim stepped out.

He took in what was happening, and he saw a look in Sam's eyes that he didn't like. He noticed the guy with the Cowboys cap standing up with his hand on his pistol and they made eye contact. Nobody moved for a few seconds and then the Cowboys cap guy said, "Hey now, everybody calm down. I just wanna have a drink and talk to this pretty woman here."

The Emmylou Harris song in the background faded into the Highwaymen and the Cowboys cap guy lurched at Sam and took out his gun. Before Sam could blink, the older woman next to the slot machines unsheathed a knife from her belt and threw it at the guy with great speed and skill. In less than an instant his pistol was on the ground and a knife was sticking through his hand.

He yelped like a trapped beaver as blood covered his hand and trickled onto the linoleum. The woman walked straight up to him and stared at him with no expression on her face. She grabbed his wrist with one hand and removed the knife from his flesh with her other. Still blank-faced, she cleaned the blade on his orange tank top, glanced at Sam and then walked out the door.

Sam stood by the bar, stunned at what had occurred. Jim took the cash that she was holding, went over to their booth and tossed it on the table. The Cowboys cap guy held his bloody palm and grimaced at them.

"This why they used to not let Indians into bars!" The guy yelled, staring at Jim. "Taking our women-ahh-"

He was interrupted when Sam suddenly walked right up to him and kicked him in the balls. His screams pitched higher and his body wilted as he fell to his knees.

Sam walked back to Jim, took his hand, and led him out the door.

"Let's get out of here," she said, standing next to the bike.

Jim nodded.

Sam put her purse in the left saddle bag, pulled her hair back and re-tied her bandana before strapping on her helmet.

As Jim started up the engine he noticed that the Ironhead 900 was gone.

Sam hopped on the back of the bike first and Jim followed. She wrapped her thighs around his hips and clung onto him a little tighter than she had before. They then got back on highway 50, and rode west.

They traveled on through long sweeping valleys that were broken up only with the occasional rusted out car or abandoned barn on the brink of collapse. There were daunting majestic mountains always in view and always seemingly distant, invariably in the background no matter how many miles of dead straight highway they covered. A side wind started up in sporadic gusts that caused huge tumbleweeds to blow across the road, narrowly missing the bike more than a few times.

They were in remote country. Harsh landscape with suffocating heat and high elevation, Ely a hundred miles behind and the next dink town a hundred miles ahead. Jim felt Sam's soft fingers holding his abdomen, and her head resting against his muscled back. It was in moments like this that Jim felt the great gulf that separated them was bridged, and made his feelings toward her seem all the more real. She had not descended to him, but it was he who had been caught up in the clouds and carried to her, and he knew he could die happy just savoring the feeling of her arms and cheek pressing against him.

There had not been a single sign of human existence for dozens of miles, so it especially caught Jim's attention when he noticed a figure on the side of the road in the distance. He slowed down as they drew closer, and saw that the figure was next to a motorcycle and looking distressed. Despite their time constraints, Jim couldn't in good conscience not at least check on the situation, as he knew there was nothing in every direction for miles. He pulled over. Sam understood what he was doing and didn't say anything. She admired his good nature, and she felt her trust in him building and her feelings for him growing.

He stepped off his bike and walked toward the solitary figure. It didn't take long for him to realize that the bike was the Ironhead Harley, and the rider was none other than the knife throwing woman from back in Ely.

"Trouble?" Jim asked as he approached.

"Shift lever broke off," she said. "Tumbleweed."

"What?" Jim asked, startled. For a second he thought that she was calling him by his name, but then, noticing the twigs stuck in the spokes, he realized she was describing a collision she had with a runaway sagebrush. "Got anybody comin?"

"No just me."

Jim knelt next to her bike to investigate her problem, turning his back to the swift breeze. Sure enough, broken off at the pinch bolt, her gear lever was gone. He figured that hitting a massive dead plant at 90 miles an hour had caused her to react so harshly that she had inadvertently kicked off her poorly designed, or poorly fastened shifter.

"Hang on," he yelled through the howl of a wind gust before running back to his bike, and to Sam.

"It's the lady from the bar isn't it?" Sam asked as she stood leaning with her hands against the handlebars of the Scout and viewing the woman and her Harley from about ten yards away. Jim nodded and popped the seat off to access his tools.

"No cell service out here," he said as he took a black pouch from its compartment under the upholstery and kneeled down.

"Yeah, none for me," she said as she held her phone up in the enormous sky. "You gonna be able to help?"

"Think I have to. If I don't she's gonna be stuck out here," he said as he used a wrench to remove the back heel shift lever, directly above the left floorboard. Jim's motorcycle was equipped with toe and heel levers, attached separately, and he decided he didn't need both.

"You can still shift without that thing?" She asked as she gazed at the way the muscles in his arms were flexing as he twisted the wrench up and down repeatedly.

"Yeah."

"Just squeeze the clutch and go up with your toes?" she asked, standing over him and placing her fingers on the left grip of the handlebars.

"Yeah," he said again, before looking up at her and smiling at the sweetness of the way she spoke. "Down to get into first, up one into neutral, and then up again into second. You want me to teach you to ride?"

She shrugged and came closer.

"Probably too heavy for me," she said as she gently brushed her leg against his shoulder. Just the slightest touch from her seemed to say a hundred words and it sent a wonderful shiver through his body.

"If you can ride a horse, I bet you could ride this," he said beholding her with his eyes, her hair blowing in the wind beneath her bandana against a fiery orange dome of heavens. His heart suddenly felt several pounds lighter and he smiled in amusement at his own emotions and shook his head, before turning his full attention back to his task. Once he finished removing the heel shaft, he lifted himself up and walked it over to the woman, along with two crescent wrenches.

"I think this might work," he said as he crouched down again next to her Harley. The woman peered over his shoulder, investigating what he was doing, and she noticed the tattoo on his arm.

"You're an Iron Raider."

Jim stopped for a moment and looked up. "Not anymore," he said before going on to tighten the bolt. He finished attaching the heel peg and wiggled it aggressively to make sure it held strong. He then stood up and tested it with his foot, before looking at her again. She had her back turned and she was gazing at the horizon. He saw the colors she was wearing and the red and grey lettering of the large patch on the back of her vest. "Redspirit?"

She turned around. "First nations Great Basin."

"Never heard of Redspirit."

She looked at him inquisitively as Sam began to make her way toward them. "You've got indigenous blood in you," the woman said as she studied Jim's face. "I'm going to a prayer ride in Willits, California."

"Prayer ride?"

"New Chapter," she said as she continued to stare at him. "Where you headed?"

"West," said Jim as Sam came and stood next to him.

"I want to thank you," Sam said to the woman as the wind continued to pick up. "For what you did back there."

The woman nodded, but said nothing.

"What's 13 and half?" Jim asked as he investigated some of the writing on her cut. Outlaw motorcycle clubs always say 1 percent somewhere in their colors, next to their patch, but on this woman's colors, it said 13 and half instead.

Her slightly wrinkled mouth formed a thin smile. "It's what we think of American justice. Live a righteous way, never put ourselves in the position of being judged by 12 jurors, 1 judge and half a chance," she said. "What are your names?"

Sam looked at Jim as if she was wondering if it was okay to answer.

"Jim."

"Sam."

"Resolve with peace, and travel in peace Jim and Sam."

"Look!" Sam said, pointing to her left. Jim turned. A herd of pronghorn antelope appeared seemingly out of nowhere and were crossing the highway. They hopped and scampered their way passed, graceful elegant creatures gliding like phantoms in staggering numbers. Two by two they made their way from south to north, disappearing into the horizon of the Dixie Valley with the Washoe Zephyr. When Jim and Sam finally turned back, the woman and the Ironhead 900 were gone. Like she was never there.

They continued west on highway 50. The hours passed and the miles flew by until they, at long last, stopped at a Flying J's outside of the town of Fallon. Jim filled the gas tank and rode over to an isolated parking spot where Sam was waiting.

"It will be dark soon," he said after stepping off the bike. "We should probably start keepin an eye out for a motel," he added, glancing at his phone and putting it back in his pocket. "I'll go get some more water, want anything from inside?"

"Yeah maybe an iced tea and something to snack on," she said, seated on the curb. She had been staring at her phone, scrolling through the missed calls and the dozens of unread texts. Karsten was apparently still alive and had been messaging her obsessively. Friends were telling her that her apartment and car had made the Fox10 Phoenix News, and they were wondering if she was okay. She contemplated whether they really cared or if they just wanted some gossip to spread around. She thought about how a crisis always seems to bring to light just how many things in a person's life are meaningless, and consequently, what's important comes to the forefront. "I'm not picky," she said.

He smiled and walked away toward the travel center. He came back a few minutes later with a plastic grocery bag full of bottled water, ice tea, a pocket cherry pie, a concha and a packaged donut. He sat down beside her.

"How far is Verdi?" she asked.

He thought about it off the top of his head as he placed the iced tea on the asphalt next to her. "Maybe another hour."

"I think I found a place for us," she said with delight, still staring at her cell phone screen.

"A motel?"

"No, it's a cabin, Airbnb."

He took a big long sip of his bottled water. "Air b&b?"

"Yeah, it's super cute, you think it will be okay?" she asked, showing him a picture. "You just get so much more for the price."

"Where is it on the map, how you pay for it?"

"I got it," she said, flipping her screen, displaying the location. She then paused and bit her lip. "They wouldn't be trying to trace my credit card would they?"

"No, they're not that smart," he said, smirking slightly from the side of his mouth. "But I can pay."

"No please, I got it, you've been paying for everything," she said, placing her hand on his wrist.

"Your Dad paid for everything."

"Well then just give me cash later."

"Donut?"

"Sure."

She took the plastic wrapped bavarian creme pastry from his hand and tore it open.

"Gas station donut," he said with a sheepish compulsion. "That okay?"

"I'm not complaining."

She took a bite, reached over and attempted to open her tea, and then gave it to him.

"You gettin enough to drink?" he asked as he unscrewed the cap and handed it back to her.

She finished chewing. "Probably not, but I don't want to have to go pee all the time," she said before taking a sip.

"You need to stay hydrated though."

She rolled her eyes at him. "I'm drinking now aren't I?"

He smiled and took another sip of water and drew his eyes ahead toward the far-reaching landscape in front of them. "Looks Full."

She followed his gaze. Still daylight, the moon was already out and low in the horizon, a perfect circle with a reddish glow in the dimming sky. "Oh my goodness, that's beautiful."

He delighted in the way she appreciated with such awe. "Let me see where this place is again." He leaned closer so he could see her phone showing the map. "I guess if we don't get there before dark we'll be able to find our way by the light of the moon."

"Sounds romantic."

He looked toward the south and west. "As long as those clouds ain't comin for us."

"Whoa, you think it will rain?"

He shrugged. "Monsoon maybe."

"Might cool us down at least, I'm still pretty warm." She took another bite of her donut and ate silently for a moment. "What do you think happened to that woman?"

"Don't know, guess we was too fascinated by them pronghorns, maybe she disappeared with them," he murmured, half-joking.

"What's that? You're mumbling."

He wrinkled his brows at her mockingly and then his cheeks dimpled as he observed her soft, delicate facial features and the adoring look she was giving him."Nothin."

Her expression charmed brightly. "What?" she asked, her voice lowering to a sensual coo.

"I was just thinkin," he said in a slow whisper, looking at her unfiltered and direct. "Who are you and where did you come from?"

Her eyes softened and she surprised him by resting her head on his shoulder.

He could smell the cheap sunscreen she had so liberally lathered on her skin, but its scent to him was like the most expensive and wonderful perfume in the world.

"I was thinking the same thing…about you. Just one full day on a motorcycle and I feel like I've known you forever somehow," she said.

No other words needed to be spoken. They sat leaning against each other, and they sat like that for a long time, watching the sun disappear and the clouds turn black above endless mountains.

"You should wear the jacket just in case," he said.

"What about you?"

"Ahh, I'll be fine, but…we better go." He stood up and reached his hand out to help her to her feet. "Lemme see that map again."

"Not too far is it?" she asked, showing him her phone one more time and pressing her shoulder softly into his chest in the process.

"It's perfect," he whispered.

"Where you at?" Snod asked over the phone as Boone sat, still in the passenger seat of the cargo van, with Billy Coxwain driving.

"We're close," Boone said, as he noticed a tumbleweed rolling across the road in front of them. "Rollin up on Fallon, tracker says he's only 50 miles or so in front of us."

"Good," Snod said before the phone went silent.

"Yo, you there Prez?"

"I keep looking at this map of Popeye's and uh…" Snod started to say.

"What?"

"We might need more info."

"What you mean?" Boone asked as he talked with his cordless headphones in his ears.

"I mean we might need to find the girl," Snod said. "Need her to help me figure out what some of this Popeye jibber jabber is supposed to mean. Bronson sent some boys up to look for her at that ranch she works at, trying to squeeze some blonde woman there about where she might have run off to."

"She's probably scared to death," Boone said.

"Who, the blonde lady?"

"No, Popeye's daughter."

"You think she might still be with Tumbleweed?"

"Don't know, but I guess that be the first place to look."

119

"Crunch em for everything he's got," Snod said. "If she ain't wit em though, then uh…I may need him to translate what this map mean, he knew the old man better than anyone."

"Right, where you is now?"

"Barstow, it's hotter than a habanero here, feel like I'm in somebody's mouth, Glub Bubber already died."

"Glub's dead?"

"Yeah, heat stroke or a heart attack or something," Snod said. "Rest stop off of the 40 and he just keeled over it was so blam-jamed hot. Somebody will have to go get em at some point, bring his body back for Mrs. Bubber."

"Looks like it might rain up here," Boone said as he viewed the ominous clouds ahead.

"Get Tumbleweed, find the girl, and then head for Willits off the 101, we'll meet you there."

"And if the girl ain't with him?"

"Then bring him to me, and hope he knows what a wishing tree is," said Snod before ending the call.

Boone put his phone on his lap and turned to his left to look at the magnificent sight of the huge orange moon laying low on the Nevada horizon. "Are you seeing this moon right now Billy?"

Billy had both hands on the wheel and was looking straight ahead. "Nope."

The sky opened up, but it wasn't rain, it was hail. Big hard hail that was pummeling Jim and Sam as they rode. It hurt bad, and Jim, wearing only a t-shirt, thought for sure that his arms would be covered in welts by the time they reached the cabin, but he couldn't do anything about it. It would do no good to pull over, there was no cover, no shelter, all he could do was just keep on going, and he was glad that he had given his jacket to Sam. He concentrated, ignoring the pain and navigating carefully over the slippery road. He squeezed Sam's thigh behind him, as if to let her know that he was going to keep her safe and it would be okay.

The temperature took a dramatic drop at almost 6,000 feet of elevation. Thunder rumbled from above and bolts of lightning flashed down as they moved through Reno, and it continued when they exited highway 80 and turned onto an old country road which clung to the Truckee River just outside of Verdi. Jim followed the meandering route until he saw a sign for River Pines Drive which he remembered from the map on Sam's phone.

He took a right. The pavement turned to gravel and continued to wind along the river for just over a mile as the sky went from day to night, until the road ended in front of a log cabin that looked straight out of a black gesso Bob Ross painting. It was lonely and outlying, enclosed with evergreens, next to the mild rapids of the river, and softly illuminated by the moonlight shining through a gap in the clouds.

"How do we get in?" Jim shouted over the now pouring rain as he stepped off the bike.

"I'll get it," Sam yelled. "She said the key would be under the mat!"

She scampered toward the front entrance, found the key and unlocked the door and Jim followed close behind, both of them desperate to get out of the elements as well as their wet clothes. They entered, kicked off their waterlogged boots, flipped on the light switches and found their way into the kitchen.

"Whoa," Jim said, running his hands over his hail beaten thighs and arms. "Are you okay?"

"I'm totally soaked," she said as she took off the jacket and flung it over a chair next to an oak countertop, where Jim tossed the keys to the Indian. "I'm cold, you must be freezing."

She was in a state of delirium. Fear and worry had dissolved in her subconscious, leaving nothing but primal urges of warmth and shelter and safety, yet she felt more alive than she thought possible.

"Where's the shower?" Jim asked as he looked around and then headed down the hall. Sam shadowed him as he entered a sort of master bedroom where he found the bath and turned the shower head faucet on as hot as it would go. "I'll let you get out of those clothes and warm up."

She looked at him blankly for less than a second before she grabbed his arm to keep him from leaving. He stopped and gazed at her with burning eyes in a way that made her feel like she had always been asleep, and now life was rubbing at her doors. Her head told her that she wanted to go back to sleep and lock her bolts in place, while her heart felt like it was throbbing and urging her to open wide and let this deliciously strange visitor enter in.

Her actions had passed beyond control of her will as his hand caressed down her rain drenched hair and to the bare flesh of her shoulder. She waited its slow progress in a torment of delight as her lips burned and her pulse leaped. She could wait no more. She stepped forward and her lips slipped against his.

He kissed her back, softly, and gently while she fought to remove his shirt which was soaked through and tight on his skin. They alternated between kissing and stripping off their clothes until they were naked. It was madness, but Sam refused to consider it madness. She was no longer herself but a woman, with a woman's carnal need. Jim did not speak. He gazed with hungry yearning at her, drinking in her loveliness and marveling that he had found himself in such a situation. It was too wonderful to be anything but a dream. His 24 years of beaten down and repressed emotions were flooding out of him all at once as he intertwined himself so effortlessly with the curves of her body and soft feminine spirit; while she who had never warmed to actual love before in her 23 years, was aware that she was warming now, and her body felt hot, well before she stepped through the sliding glass door onto the glossy tile floor beneath the now steamy shower.

"Gimmie another one a them macadillos," Flash said, leaning forward as Billy drove on an old country road that clung to the Truckee River.

"There macadamias," Boone said as he finished chewing.

"Yeah that's what I said, macadamios," Flash said. "What he doin way out here anyway?"

"Take a right take a right!" Boone said, turning to Billy as he gave Flash the bag of nuts. He looked hard at his phone and noticed the sign for River Pines Drive.

"You sure?" Billy asked with skepticism, surprised by how far out in the sticks they were.

Boone looked at his phone again, it was signaling for them to go even deeper into the wilderness in order to meet with the tracking device. "Yeah pretty sure."

Billy turned the wheel.

"Gotta get more a these macadillos," Flash said.

"Nice they left us those," Jim said as he looked up at Sam. She was standing in the kitchen nibbling on a chocolate chip cookie, one of many which had been left for them on a plastic wrapped paper plate by the homeowners.

"They're delicious, you should have some," she said with a giggle as she grabbed another and sauntered toward him. Jim was sitting on a couch in the corner of the main living room, next to a wood pellet stove that was just starting to heat up and beginning to dry their clothes which were hanging over some chairs nearby. It really wasn't all that cold in the house, but it was still stormy outside and the stove was comforting.

"Okay," he said as she handed it to him and lowered herself down on the couch beside him and threw a red cashmere blanket over her naked legs. He took a sip of the hot herbal tea she had made him and then took a bite of the cookie. She leaned against him and wrapped her arms around his shoulders.

Now that they were dry and warm they were able to fully appreciate the charm of the cabin. It was a dream of a place, tiny, but exceedingly quaint in a rustic way. There were copper bottomed pots and pans dangling beneath maplewood cabinets, Navajo style rugs hung on

125

the walls like tapestries and there was an upright piano and a classical guitar on a stand in the corner.

"Do you ever dream about, what you want to do…who you wanna be?" she asked him after a long moment of silence.

Jim looked at her and thought about it hard, nobody had ever asked him a question like that before. "Uh, don't really know," he said before taking another sip of tea. "Maybe just, be a part of something good, or build something. It's just that I think that maybe I've been in a…in a…what's the word? In association with something bad my whole life, I'd like to change that, really see if I can make something of myself."

He instantly felt stupid and unsure if he had answered her question properly, or if he was making sense. All of his childhood had been troubled by a vague unrest. He never had a dream, or known what he wanted, but he had wanted something that he had searched vainly for until he met the girl that he was looking at, and now his unrest had become sharp and he knew at last, with crystal clarity, that what he wanted and dreamed of most of all, was love. "What uh, what about you?" he asked.

She gazed at him inquisitively and he wondered if she could read his thoughts. "Well I've always wanted to teach riding, horses…maybe take tourists on trail rides on a beach somewhere, actually own a horse or two, start a business," she said. "I mean, it's just a dream, but…"

"You really do miss the ocean don't you."

She sipped her tea. "Yeah, there's something so peaceful and calming about it."

"That's where we'll be, the ocean, come this time tomorrow."

She ran her fingers through her still damp hair and turned toward him. "What are we going to do when we get there?"

"Well you know about this wishing tree and they won't right?"

"Yeah."

"So we'll just try and sneak over there, stay out of sight and uh…"

"Dig with picks and shovels?" she said before laughing.

"Maybe, I guess we won't know til we see it. You nervous?"

She flashed him a stunning white smile. "I was," she said in a slow whisper. "But somehow, not anymore."

He smiled back. "I know what you mean."

The wood stove was making the room very warm and Sam removed the blanket from her lap, exposing the soft flesh of her thighs. She noticed the way his eyes swept over her like he could not understand what was happening. Like what he was seeing was too wonderful to be anything but hallucinations, and she thrilled with these proofs of her power that proclaimed her a woman, and she took a certain delight in playfully tormenting him.

"What?" she asked finally, as she felt like his handsome stare could burn holes through her eyes. She almost knew what he was thinking but she wondered if he would say it.

His lips contorted into a smirk but he said, "Nothin."

They held each other's gaze for a long moment, and her lips waxed sultry.

"Still wondering who you are and where you come from," he said at last.

She smiled, and unconsciously batted her long eyelashes. "Well, I'm half Spanish, if you really want to know."

He cleared his throat. "Tell me...tell me more about your mother."

She let out a small sigh. "She was a very classy lady," she said, leaning forward. "Dad met her in the courtyard just outside of Basilica de la Sagrada Familia, when he was starting up a new chapter for the Iron Raiders in Barcelona, or so I was told."

"Did you grow up there, in Spain?"

"No, somehow my dad got my mom to move to California, and after they divorced, my mom sort of fell in love with Sedona and took me with her...umm, what about you?"

"What about me?"

She nodded slow, while keeping her vision focused on his eyes. "Your mother and father."

"Not much to tell," he said. "Never knew my mother, was raised mostly by my great aunt. My father died when I was 10, and uh, I was, I grew up on the Yurok Indian Reservation, and, just ran away...after he died."

There was a pause, elevating the crackle and popping noise of the pellet stove. "Is your great aunt, still...around?"

She noticed his uncomfortableness with her questions as well as the way his eyes were drifting toward the guitar on a stand to his right. She decided to change the subject, to something perhaps less emotional.

"You know how to play that?" she asked.

He smiled, leaned forward and picked it up. He adjusted himself in his seat and ran his thumb down on each nylon string individually. He carefully turned each peg on the headstock until he felt it was in tune enough for him to play her something. She watched him curiously and listened attentively as his fingers moved skillfully up and down the neck and a beautiful soft romantic sound was released into their cozy cabin. The melody was haunting and heart wrenching, and her eyebrows raised with delight and her lips moved into the shape of an 'O' when he started serenading her in Spanish.

"El español...es la lengua amorosa," he sang in a soothing voice as his fingers continued to pick and pluck at the strings in perfect harmony. She listened to his song, quietly and carefully and when he was finished she clapped.

"That was amazing," she said as pleasure and wonder streamed through her eyes and lips. "You are full of surprises."

"Did you understand the words?"

"It's a very sad song," she whispered. She turned, gazed over at the Steinway and stood up. "Now it's my turn. It's been a while and I have nails so no making fun."

"I don't know how you work with horses with those nails."

She gave him a twinkling little look. "I'm a bit of a walking contradiction."

She sat down, the rickety old wood of the piano bench creaking beneath her. She lifted the fallboard, arched her back and began to play and sing, 'Will You Love Me Tomorrow'. Her voice was shy, yet as lovely as she, and her fingers danced along the keys and her posture slumped and swayed with the emotion of the tune. She sang with fervor and passionate sorrow, and Jim who was remarkably susceptible to music, found that the sight and sound of her playing had fired him to audacities of feeling, flooded his mind with beauty and loosened romance from deep within his soul. About halfway through, he began to finger the guitar in tender accompaniment.

Billy drove the van slowly on the gravel road, and even slower still once the little cottage was in view.

"That's his bike," Flash said as he pointed from between the front seats at the motorcycle that was getting rained on in front of the cabin.

"Indian," Billy said as he eased the vehicle closer.

"Yeah," Flash said as he shoved a handful of macadamias into his mouth and chewed like a wood chipper.

"Okay okay, shhh, y'all know what to do," Boone said, putting his phone in the glove compartment and pulling out a compact disc, Face Value.

"Can't wait," Flash said with his mouth still full of nuts as he held a roll of heavy duty duct tape and unspooled it a few inches, making that distinctive tearing sound.

Billy stopped the van but kept it running and Boone inserted the disc into the CD player. He turned the volume all the way up, started with track one, and pressed play. A booming thunder rolled and rumbled in the night sky and the rain continued to trickle down. Electronic drums pulsing from the van's tricked out speakers began their slow recognizable beat.

Back inside the cabin, Sam was finishing her song and asked for a final time, "Will you still love me... tomorrow?"

She then paused for a moment, and took her hands off the keys and placed them on her lap before swiveling toward Jim.

He stared at her, completely infatuated, enamored and enraptured, and answered her question by simply saying, "Yes."

He then quite abruptly, froze in place.

"What?" she asked, startled by the sudden change in his demeanor.

"You hear that?"

He held the guitar with one hand and muted the strings, his face racked with fear. They both became very still, and listened in silence. The hairs on Jim's arm stood up. The atmospheric percussive sound that was coming from the van, drowned out the rain and poured into the cabin.

"Is that...music from outside?" Sam asked as her eyes got big.

Jim's face drained of color. He knew exactly what was happening. He knew the Iron Raider's flair for the dramatic and he knew the use of that particular song meant that a raid was about to occur and all hell was going to break loose. He also knew exactly how much time he had to figure out what to do, 3 minutes and 41 seconds.

"It's them," he whispered, jolting to his feet and setting the guitar down. He stopped for a second and grabbed the clothes which were now mostly dry, cradled them with one arm and took Sam by the hand. "Come on!"

They ran down the hall toward the bedroom. "Shoes!" he said as he halted and grabbed Sam's boots while his other hand held her clothes. They then scampered around the corner to the bathroom where there was a small walk-in closet. Jim swung open the door and they went in together. There was a tight little nook behind the door that was surrounded by shelves filled with extra blankets and towels.

"Put your pants on," he said in a hushed voice as he gave her the jeans and dropped the boots. They hastily dressed themselves and then crouched down. "I don't know how but they found me," he said as he clasped her upper arms and looked her directly in the eyes. "Stay here, they can't know I'm with you, they're here for me, not you."

"What are you gonna do?" she asked, her voice wrenched in woe. They could still hear the music flooding its way into the house like a terrible ticking time bomb with each repetitive utterance of 'Oh Lord'.

"No matter what happens you need to stay here okay?" Jim said in a cadence and tone of deadly seriousness. "If you stay here I promise you'll be safe."

Her lips were quivering and her eyes were as big as saucers.

"Promise me!" he said in the loudest whisper he could muster.

She gasped. "I promise."

"The guns are still the bike." His eyes darted in frantic deliberation.

"Stay here with me!" she pleaded.

"I can't. They've already seen my motorcycle, they know I'm here and they're not going to stop until they find me."

"Well then you need to promise me something," she said, her expression growing soft. "Promise me that you'll stay alive."

She placed her hands on his wrists and he looked at her for a moment and then nodded his head unconvincingly, before getting up, quietly shutting the closest door and leaving her alone. He slunk down the hall and turned to the front door of the house where he slipped his still damp Nokonas over his black socks.

He reversed toward a sliding glass door in the back of the cabin that led to a wooden deck, where he could hear the rapids of the river moving in the darkness. He lurked on the wooden planks and around to the side, keeping as close to the thick log walls as possible as he approached the front driveway. Peering over the corner he saw the white van with its front doors wide open. The engine was still running and the music was blaring. It was getting close.

He tilted his head over the edge of the exterior wall once more but this time he was confronted by the bruised, scarred up face of Flash Fontana. Jim shuttered at the initial shock of being only inches away from Flash and he instinctively jolted backward. Flash still had the roll of duct tape and he unripped it and stretched it out in his hands as he excitedly chased Jim to the front of the cabin near the van.

Jim stopped running once he got out on the gravel driveway. Fleeing the scene would be too risky, as it may result in them searching the cabin and finding Sam, he thought.

He looked left and he looked right. He saw that there were now two of them. It was Boone Dix. If straight ahead of Jim was twelve on a clock, then Flash was at ten, and Boone was at two. Flash with his tape, and Boone with his switchblade. Jim was surprised that the Mauser P38 Boone carried was still holstered, but that didn't make his knife look any less troublesome. Jim dug his boots into the ground as the rain continued to plaster his hair to his forehead. He listened to the famous song coming from the van, hearing the echoing of 'I remember, don't worry.' It was very near, if it even mattered anymore.

"Where's the girl?" Boone asked, shouting over the music and rainfall.

"She's long gone," Jim yelled. "She don't care about no treasure, and neither do I. Why don't you just let me go?"

"No can do Tumbleweed," Flash said with a gaping smile. "Once a Raider, always a Raider."

"How'd you find me?" Jim asked as his eyes shifted back and forth from Flash to Boone. The music from the van seemed to be getting louder.

"You can't fool me," Boone said.

"Letter of Marque," Flash said.

They stared at each other. All three standing silent in a moment of excruciating tension as the words, 'No stranger to you and me,' came from the van's speakers.

Then it dropped. The famous drum fill pounded away and Boone charged Jim with the knife held high in his right hand, while Flash came at him with his spool of tape. Boone thrust his blade toward Jim's left shoulder. Jim stomped on Boone's right foot as he ran and braced his thigh against his left knee. Boone's leg buckled while Jim blocked the stab attempt with his forearm and encouraged Boone's momentum in the direction it wanted to go, and in so doing, caused Boone's leg to snap at the knee and fold back on itself in a way that no knee should ever bend. Boone screamed and fell forward on his face, onto the hard packed, weather soaked ground. Then Jim's eyes went dark.

Jim didn't know it yet, but it was Billy Coxwain. Billy had snuck up on him from behind and stuffed a black bag, designed for a motorcycle helmet, over Jim's head while Flash Fontana quickly sealed it tight by wrapping the tape around his neck.

Billy shoved Jim's face down on the gravel and pinned him to the ground by pressing his knee into his spine. He then grabbed Jim's arms and held them against his back while Flash quickly bound them together with more tape, and then proceeded to do the same thing to his ankles. Boone Dix was still lying face down and he was screeching and muttering in extreme agony. Billy looked at him and noticed that his foot was turned in the opposite direction of his other foot and his jeans had turned a much darker color in the area around his knee. Flash finished his tape job, stood up and kicked Jim hard in the stomach and then once more in the head while Billy cleared out of the way.

"How do you like me now!" Flash yelled before kicking him once again.

"Stop," Billy said as he watched Jim squirm and flop, unable to move his limbs. "Go check out the house."

Flash sneered at Billy and then turned toward the cabin. He kicked Jim in the back one more time before he walked to the front door.

Billy crouched down and put his head near where he thought Jim's ear was.

"You wasn't with nobody right?" he asked as he shoved his leg into his back once again.

Jim twisted and grunted against the hard packed pieces of shale beneath him. "No!" he said in a gasp of a voice.

"You know what a wishing tree is?"

Billy pressed him harder.

Jim grimaced under the bag on his head and thought for a moment. His mind was going crazy thinking about Flash finding Sam in the closet and all the things he might do to her. He suddenly realized why Boone had come at him with a knife instead of just shooting him. It was because they thought that they needed him alive, and Jim started to put some pieces together.

"Yeah, I know what the wishing tree is!" he said in a convulsing rasp.

"What is it?"

"It's a...it's a special tree,...uh, everyone knows, where I come from," Jim said, panting. "A tree, uhhh, sacred to my people," he lied.

"You know how to find it?"

"I can show you where it is," Jim said as he fidgeted around beneath the pressure of Billy's body. "But you gonna need to get Boone some medical attention, or he gonna lose that leg."

Billy, again pushed into Jim, but he did look over at Boone's knee. He leaned forward and lightly touched the area of discoloration on Boone's jeans. It was soaking wet, and not from the rain. The music in the van faded out and the next song began.

"Oh bother," Billy muttered under his breath. "Don't move!" he yelled as he rose to his feet to turn the music off.

Flash was inside the cabin. He saw the fire of the pellet stove burning in the living room and he looked around.

"If anybody's in here you best come out now," he shouted.

Sam was still in the closet on the other side of the house, but she could hear the man loud and clear and she shuttered, wondering who he might be. The horrors of seeing her apartment and her flaming car came back to her, and she crouched down lower and covered herself with one the blankets from the shelving. She took her phone from the pocket of her jeans, there was no service so far out in the woods. She heard footsteps pounding and growing increasingly louder with each terrifying thud. A man's boot on creaky hardwood floors.

"Come out come out wherever you are!" the voice said, this time much more boisterous and close. The pounding footsteps continued. "I find you…"

The voice now sounded like it was coming from just behind the door, suddenly so frighteningly loud that it was all she could do not to scream. It was so close she could actually hear him breathing.

"Hey!" a voice yelled, this time a different voice, much deeper than the other one. "Boone is in pretty bad shape, we best git outta here."

"Who made you coach?" the other voice said. "I wanna find that girl bro."

"The kid's gonna lead us to that wish tree, he knows. Come on there's nobody here, we gots ta go. Need you to set Boone's leg, if she's as pretty as you say she is, she ain't gonna be hangin out with no halfbreed anyhow, let's git!"

Sam listened with her fingers crossed as she heard the footsteps behind the door shuffle around and grow ever fainter. She vaguely made out the sounds of men grunting in the distance several moments later and then she thought she heard car doors shutting, followed by, nothing.

There was complete silence, deafening silence, and her fear began to turn to sorrow. It was only minutes ago that she had her arms wrapped around Jim's shoulders, only minutes ago that she was sitting next to the warm stove watching while he was so beautifully serenading her with the guitar, and now there was nothing, only silence. She curled herself into a ball, closed her eyes and prayed it was all just a horrible dream.

*"I don't know her now
my bitter pill, my broken vow
this girl, this bird who sings
she remembers everything."*

It was hours before Sam finally worked up the courage to get up and leave the safety of her cocoon of a closet, but she did. She tiptoed into the bedroom and listened for signs of life. She crept her way around the hall and then stopped to see if she could hear anything, still nothing. She went to the front door and opened it slowly, the motorcycle was still in the driveway, but that was it.

Stepping outside she looked around. The rain had stopped and the moon was high. Everything seemed calm. It was total darkness and not a sound could be heard with the exception of the river and the sporadic hooting of an owl. She ran toward the motorcycle and searched the saddlebags until she found the 38 special revolver. She took it and cried out into the night sky.

"Jim!" she yelled. "Jim!" she yelled again, this time in almost a wail as she held the gun with both hands, no response. She ran back inside and called his name a third time to no avail.

She collapsed on the sofa next to the still burning stove, wrapped herself in the cashmere blanket and rocked forward and back nervously with the pistol held tightly in her grasp, her wrist dangling over bent knees, hands trembling. She didn't move from that spot until she saw the light of the early morning dawn begin to pour through the windows.

She made herself get up. She walked to the kitchen and noticed the keys to Jim's motorcycle were still where he left them, on the oak countertop. She paused for a moment and stared at them before running outside. The motorcycle was still there, just as it had been during the night.

"Jim!" she yelled. Still nothing.

She investigated the saddlebags again. There were some extra pairs of socks, a t-shirt, Jim's briefs, her sunscreen and hand lotion, a few bottles of water, phone chargers, and the Sig Sauer 1911. She grabbed one of the chargers, closed up the saddlebags and started to walk back toward the house, and then stopped. She stood still for a moment, turned around and went back to the bike.

Looking down at the gear lever above the left foot floorboard, she swung her leg over the seat and sat down. She stuffed the charger in the front pocket of her jeans and placed her fingers on the handlebars and tilted the bike off its kickstand. The seat was low enough and her legs were long enough that she could easily reach both of her boots down to the gravel and place them flat and firm on the ground. She balanced the bike, testing its weight by carefully teetering it from side to side. She felt its heaviness and lowered it back onto its stand. She went back inside.

"Wake up!" said a mean sounding voice as Jim's eyes sprung open after a hand hit him in the face. He blinked as he adjusted to the morning light and realized he was in the van and his wrists and ankles were still bound with tape. He looked up from his laying down position and he saw the tiny head atop the oversized neck that belonged to Flash Fontana. He was so close that Jim could smell Flash's breath, and it was so foul that Jim wished he still had that bag over his head. Then there was a sudden and excruciating pain. Jim grimaced, yelled and jolted his neck back and saw that Flash was now holding a strip of duct tape in his hand, the strip that he had just ripped from Jim's mouth.

"That'll jump start your day better than coffee," Flash said with a laugh. "Boone ain't lookin so hot, you needa fix em."

Jim grunted and shifted in agony, he was on hard metal, his feet pointed toward the middle and front seats of the van and his head near the doors in the back. His entire body felt stiff and sore and now his lips felt like they were on fire. "I ain't a doctor," he gasped.

"You broke em' you fix him!" Flash said before he looked over his shoulder as if he was afraid of being seen.

144

"I told you, he needs real medical attention," Jim said.

"His leg is starting to stink!"

"He needs a hospital, probably has gangrene by now."

"Gangrene?" Asked Flash, confused. "We don't have time for a hospital and this is your screw up."

The two men stared at each other silently. Jim started to squirm and then struggled to sit up. He looked at Flash, dumbfounded. "You gonna take me to him?"

"Oh, yeah," Flash said finally.

He took a knife and cut the tape around Jim's ankles, grabbed his arm and yanked him out of the back of the van. Jim staggered to his feet. They were at a single story strip of a motel that looked sketchy even by Iron Raider standards. Jim thought he could've walked out of that van with the black sack still taped over his head and nobody around that place that might have seen him would've thought twice about it.

"He felt the muzzle of a handgun press into his back as Flash walked him toward the building.

"Try anything fancy, and you're a deadman," Flash said.

Jim smiled to himself. In a way he felt almost invincible, but he wasn't ready to call Flash's bluff just yet.

Flash banged on the door to the motel room and Billy Coxwain opened it up. They entered and Flash pushed Jim toward the bed where Boone Dix was laid up. Jim turned around, saw Billy deadbolt the door as well as Flash still pointing his Czech Republic made Alien pistol in his direction. Jim, with his hands bound behind his back, drew his attention to Boone.

He had set Boone's leg the night before, albeit hastily in the van in his bewildered state, and he had wrapped the knee excessively with the gauze that Billy had purchased at a drugstore somewhere near Truckee. Jim had tied off Boone's thigh with a bungee cord and had helped them make a splint out of a lever-action Winchester rifle.

"You're lucky Prez wants you alive," Boone said in a strained wheeze of a voice. Jim could see that he wasn't looking well. His face was pale and sweaty and his lower leg had turned so blue it was almost black.

"Shhh, try not to talk," Jim said with more than a hint of sarcasm.

"You're the wagon burner," Billy said. "Do some medicine man healing or whatever you people do."

Jim tilted his head in amusement. These men really did seem to think that he had some kind of knowledge or ability to heal, while in reality all Jim knew was that Boone needed a hospital if he was going to keep his leg, or possibly his life.

"Untie me."

Billy looked at Flash and Flash reluctantly put his gun down and proceeded to cut the tape around Jim's hands with his knife.

"Do you have any alcohol?" Jim asked with arms now free.

The two men behind him looked at each other before Billy grabbed a half-empty bottle of whiskey and tossed it at Jim.

Jim unscrewed the cap, took in the cheap ethanol smell and his mouth watered, but he resisted. "Drink this," he said as he carefully brought it to Boone's lips.

"And then what?" Flash asked with concern.

Jim thought about it. His mind had been haunted with nothing but visions of Sam since he had been driven off in the van the night before. His heart ached more than his face and body and he was filled with wonderment as to what she might be going through or feeling, and all he could think of was getting back to her, somehow, someway. Flash had already smashed his phone to pieces with the butt of a gun, and Jim didn't have Sam's phone number memorized. Even if he was able to escape from these men, he wasn't sure of what he could do other than get back to his motorcycle, and back to the cabin.

"I got some healing herbs back at the bike," Jim said with his fingers figuratively crossed as he lifted his head up, still with his back to Billy and Flash.

"Nice try Tumbleweed," Flash said. "We ain't goin all the way back there, besides if that was the case why didn't ya say something before?"

"Didn't know how bad it was," Jim said, hiding his discouragement. "Bring me more of that medical tape."

Billy turned around and grabbed the roll of gauze off the dresser next to the TV and walked it up to Jim.

"You sure you know where the wish tree is?" Billy asked in a demonic whisper as he glared straight into Jim's eyes.

"Yeah," Jim said before clearing his throat. "I know where it is." He began unspooling the tape, drawing his attention back at Boone. The crippled man was still wearing his jeans, but Jim had cut them into shorts on the wounded knee side. "If he don't look better soon, I'm gonna have to slice into him."

Flash's face became panicked. "What herbs we need?"

Jim smiled, knowing he could finally use his heritage to his advantage. "My people, when uh, someone would have a broken leg," he said in his best rez accent as his mind raced to think of the words, making it all up as he went. "My uh, I mean the um, elders used to squeeze the juices of the um...prickly pear cactus over the wound."

"And that will help his leg?" Flash asked with enthusiasm as he took a step forward.

"It will help him heal, yes," Jim said as he continued to wrap tape around Boone's leg.

"There's prickly pears all around in California once we git outta these mountains," Flash said. "Let's go git it!"

Jim's smile widened.

Sam stuck the keys in the ignition of the Indian Scout, squeezed the clutch and started the engine. She pressed down on the shift lever with her left boot and realized it could not go any further. Remembering what Jim told her, she slipped her foot beneath it, lifted upward and the green light that had been on before lit up again and she released her grip from the clutch, safely in neutral.

She had on her bandana, helmet and sunglasses. She had zipped herself up in Jim's leather jacket that she wore over her camisole and the only thing she thought was missing was a pair of gloves, but nonetheless, she felt ready. She had even tied Jim's helmet to the back seat, unwilling to accept he wouldn't need it again.

The Scout purred and vibrated between her thighs and she sensed its power, much like she had sensed the power of a horse. She gripped the clutch, kicked the bike back into gear and twisted the throttle with her right hand. The machine convulsed and rocked forward. She let go of her left hand and the engine stalled and died.

Lurching to a stop she flung her feet to the ground and began tipping over. Pressing into the gravel hard with her left boot she used all the strength in her thigh to keep the bike from dropping. She told herself she could do this, told herself she had to do this and told herself she would do this. There was no other option. Carefully tilting the bike upright and balanced, she gritted her teeth, knocked it back into neutral and tried again.

She stalled once more but this time she felt more comfortable in her abilities to maintain balance. On the third try, she eased the clutch out more slowly and started moving. Figuring if she could learn to do this on gravel she would have no problem once she reached open roads. The bike continued to roll ahead in first gear and she placed both of her boots up on the floorboards. It was like western style riding, different from the English style she was used to, with her feet further forward.

She tapped it up, passed neutral, into second gear and gave the accelerator another slight twist. Her speed increased to 15 and then to almost 20 miles per hour. The sun was out, the clouds were gone, she was surrounded by bristlecone pines, fresh mountain air and for the first time since Jim disappeared, she forgot to be afraid.

She made her way to the asphalt of River Pines drive and all the way into the town of Verdi, never going past third gear. She spotted a diner called 'The Pancake Mill' and realized how hungry she was. Rolling into the parking lot, she shifted down, killed the engine and, dropped the bike.

It felt like it was happening in slow motion, tipping over surprisingly gently onto her left leg. She managed to squirm her way out from underneath it awkwardly, and unharmed, yet feeling embarrassed, attempted to lift the bike up by the handlebars. She moaned with all her strength but it was too heavy, and a huge wave of doubt and dread swept over her as she struggled to catch her breath.

"Push on the seat," a voice said.

Sam turned around and was shocked to see that the knife throwing woman from Ely, the woman whom Jim had helped on the roadside over a hundred miles ago was standing next to her. She was already gripping the handlebars of the Scout and she nodded at Sam assuredly. Sam stepped back and grabbed the middle saddle with one hand and clenched the bar beneath the rear seat backrest with the other. She bent her legs and pushed along with the woman until the bike was upright. The woman then flung the kickstand all the way forward with her foot and steadied the motorcycle down into a secure position.

"Thank you," Sam said in a breathy voice as she looked the woman over. She was so tiny. Barely five feet tall, a few inches shorter than herself and considerably lighter, but somehow she had enough strength to hoist the bike up by the handlebars without breaking a sweat.

"Where's the Yurok boy?" Sam bit her lip and the woman seemed to sense her malaise. "Were you going inside?"

Sam nodded.

"Come on, let's go," the woman said in a way that put her more at ease.

Although it was Sunday, it was still early enough that the place was relatively quiet. Sam removed her helmet and sunglasses as they went in together and were led by a hostess to a booth in the corner. It was isolated from other customers, and only the eyes of Clint Eastwood and James Dean stared at her from their picture frames on the wall as she sat down. The whole diner was decked out in pop culture, jukebox and everything.

They ordered a cup of coffee each, which was promptly delivered and Sam sat with her face buried in her hands for a long moment. She then began stirring cream and sugar into her coffee with a spoon, her hands shaking.

"What happened?" the woman asked.

Sam blinked a few times. "I don't know. Somebody found us last night, I don't know how, but they did." She paused and took her phone out of the jacket pocket.

"Somebody is tracking you," the woman said in her seemingly usual, all-knowing voice. "Who?"

Sam sighed so deeply that she sank lower in the springy laminate cushion of the booth. "The Iron Raiders, can they trace phones?"

The woman shrugged. "Doubt it."

"I'm going to try and call him. We didn't have service before."

The woman stared at her curiously as she watched her put the phone to her ear. She waited.

"It's like it's shut off or something," Sam said after a few moments, looking more than worried.

"Were they playing a certain song when they came?"

Sam bounced to attention when she heard her say that and placed her phone on the table. "Yes, they were," she said in amazement. She was beginning to wonder about this woman. This was now the third time she had seen her, and while it was plausible, it all seemed more than a coincidence. The perfectly thrown knife, the way she had disappeared like smoke out on the highway, and now, with her borderline omnipotence, making Sam contemplate whether or not she herself was even thinking rationally anymore. "How did you know that?"

"They did the same when they came for one of my brothers," said the woman after taking a sip of coffee. "They do that when someone tries to leave the club, which was what Jim was trying to do."

"One of your brothers was an Iron Raider?"

"Yes," said the woman as she ran her hand over the bronze skin of her forehead and up to her midnight black hair. "One of my riding brothers, part of our family."

Sam looked at her sadly, unsure of what to say, and then fear crept back into her mind.

"Don't worry. Jim seemed like a smart boy," she said as she looked at Sam almost maternally. "You love him don't you."

Sam smiled softly with only her eyes, and then gazed down at her fingernails, timid and guarded. "I...I don't know."

"He is in love with you. I could see it in the way he looked at you. The same look that you have now when you think of losing him. It's the look of true love, and true love cannot die."

Sam placed her hands on her coffee mug and contemplated for a long while. "I wish I believed you," she said finally, just before a server came to see if they were ready.

Despite everything, the heavenly smells coming from the kitchen made Sam's hunger pangs intolerable. She ordered french toast, scrambled eggs with hash browns and bacon, while the woman asked for a couple of the homemade almond bear claws.

Once the server had gone, Sam removed Jim's jacket and revealed herself in the top that she had been wearing now for several days in a row. She hung her head and began to feel the effects of getting no sleep the night before.

The woman studied Sam's face and appearance. Not wearing any makeup, her youthful skin and beauty still dazzled, but she looked tired and slightly older than when she had seen her last, just one day prior.

"You and Jim were running away."

Sam looked up from her nails and thought about it. She hadn't been running away, but she had been running. She stared at the woman. "I don't think I ever got your name."

"Kima."

Sam pressed her lips together and then sighed. "Thanks again for your help, this is my first time riding a motorcycle."

"Jim said that you were going west, how far are you going?"

She considered her question for a moment. Something about this woman told Sam that she could trust her. She looked her directly in the eye with a surge of determination. "The Iron Raiders are headed for the Lost Coast, I need to beat them there. If they've kidnapped Jim or something, then that's where he'll be too."

"That's the direction I'm headed, why there?"

Sam sipped her coffee, took another deep breath and set her mug back on the table. "Do you know the name Ronnie Rush? Or I mean, uh... Popeye Rush?"

Kima looked at her with suspicion. "Yes, one of my brothers rode with him."

"Um, Popeye passed away recently," Sam said as her big eyes shifted back down toward the table. "He was my father, he was killed by the Iron Raiders."

Kima furrowed her brows. "Popeye Rush was an Iron Raider," she said with certainty. "He was, the, Iron Raider."

Sam nodded. "Yeah, he was until they killed him."

"They're after his money then aren't they."

Sam gazed at her, surprised. "What makes you say that?"

"If anyone knows the name Popeye Rush, then they know the stories about his hidden treasure."

Sam leaned back with a frustrated look. "Sometimes I feel like I'm the only one who didn't know who my father was."

Kima's narrow lips almost cracked a smile. "I'm meeting up with my sisters and brothers in Willits, that's on the way to where you want to go, I'll ride with you, if you want."

Jim stared at the sleeping face of Boone Dix as they both laid flat in the back of the van. They had been sealed off from the front, as Flash didn't like the smell, and for all intents and purposes, they were alone.

Jim puzzled over just how it was that they were able to track him down, first in Jerome, and then once again in Verdi. His mouth had been resealed with tape and his hands and feet were again bound together, but he could roll over freely. He turned onto his side and his eyes were drawn toward Boone's jeans. Sticking out ever so slightly from his pocket, was the corner of a cell phone. He flipped himself so that his hands could reach it from behind his back.

The van jostled as it moved down the road at a high rate of speed, and Jim assumed they must be on interstate 80, descending into the Sacramento Valley. He moved his fingers carefully from behind his butt and discreetly removed the phone from Boone's pocket until he was holding it in his hands. He turned and glanced at Boone's pale and clammy face one more time, he was out cold.

Jim twisted his head as far around as he could over and illuminated the phone's screen. A password was required, and after nearly dislocating his shoulder, he typed out, laboriously and tediously, 'raider' and it was unlocked. He swiped his thumb over the screen, trying to check the messages but before he did, an application called 'gumshoe' caught his attention for reasons more divine than he could explain. He opened it, and contorted his head further over his shoulder to get a better look.

There was a map. He zoomed out with his fingers and saw that it centered on the middle of California and he noticed a red dot. He zoomed back in and saw that the dot was moving. He clutched the phone tighter and rolled onto his other side and closed his eyes for a moment. Turning back around and looking again, he understood. Boone had planted a bug on his motorcycle and Jim knew exactly when he did it, at his trailer the night before he left, and it all made sense now, with the exception of one thing that perplexed him, yet raised hope at the same time. If the red dot indicated the location of the Indian, why then was it on the move and advancing into the central valley. The only explanation he could think of, was Sam.

"How was that?" Kima asked after pulling into a gas station in former gold mining the town of Grass Valley.

"Great," Sam said after parking at the pump behind her. She stepped off the bike gingerly, and carefully made sure her kickstand was down and all the way forward. "It was amazing."

It was true, amazing was the best word Sam could think of to describe it, although if you asked her a hundred miles ago she would have said terrifying. Kima made her feel comfortable however, and she proved herself to be a good teacher, just as Sam proved to be a fast learner.

Having made it over the pass and into the foothills of Sierra Nevadas on the California side, they exited interstate 80 to merge onto the two lane highway 20, which would cut them toward Yuba City and bypass Sacramento. It was a magnificent ride. Sitting on the back of a motorcycle was one thing, but clasping the handlebars was a different thing entirely. Never before had Sam experienced such exhilaration and freedom. She felt empowered and in control, and her senses of sight and smell had been delightfully overwhelmed.

It was similar to the way she felt when riding a horse, and while the motorcycle could not duplicate the feeling of a living breathing animal, the animal could not duplicate the 80 miles per hour or the covering of vast distances.

They filled their tanks and pulled forward to a parking area by a curb to stretch their legs.

"You got that clutch down now," Kima said with a smile. "You're gonna be a pro by tonight."

"Yep," Sam said after taking a sip of water, remembering Jim's hydration advice. Thinking of him and where he might be caused in her an influx of melancholy. She looked down at the ground and placed her weight on one hip as her demeanor dilated with the direction of the soft summer breeze flowing through her hair. She turned to Kima. "I think I better go use the restroom."

"Yeah, I'll be right behind ya," Kima said as she lit up an oval shanked Canadian tobacco pipe.

Sam returned several minutes later with a bottled iced mocha in her hand. She walked to the bike and stood alone, waiting for Kima. She took a sip from her cold beverage and looked around. The town was born out of the California gold rush and it still had shades of the 1850s, with historical strips of adjacent brick buildings running on both sides of the narrow main road. Across the street a Union Jack flew from a pole and beneath it sat a drifter wearing a feathered war bonnet, panhandling with a paper bag covered bottle in his hand. Sam observed the foothills to the west, they were barren and burned.

"To the indigenous people, the land is sacred," Kima said, appearing beside her and following her eyes to the fire scorched trees and earth. "When the white man came looking for gold, they overused the land and created drought and starvation, and the fires just get worse every year."

159

Sam nodded.

"In the 20 years after they found the gold, 15,000 were murdered in cold blood right here, but no one calls it genocide," Kima said. "Now all we can do is help each other."

Sam felt the wind stiffen and flutter against her open jacket. "Is that why you joined Redspirit?"

"There used to be 60 million of us, now there are less than 400,000," Kima said, sticking the pipe in her mouth again. "Those of us left, definitely need to stick together, that's why all clubs and gangs are formed."

"And my father?"

"From what I have heard, I think your father wanted to live like they did in the old days, let the wild west stay wild. Some people were born to lead, some men cannot live in the white man's society. Your father was a great leader, but he started something he couldn't control."

Sam nodded again and Kima threw her leg over her bike and fired it up. Sam drank the last of her mocha and placed the bottle in the nearby recycle bin and plopped herself in her saddle. They rode off together on the 20, and blazed into the hot flat farmlands of the central valley and across interstate 5 at the town of Williams. It was smooth riding and they were making good time, arriving in the gorgeous vineyard topped rolling hills, round and bulging soft on the western side of Lake County, still with plenty of daylight ahead.

The ground beneath Jim changed from smooth asphalt to bumpy unpaved road. The rocky ride continued for a minute or so and then the van came to a stop, but the engine was left running. He was blinded by sunlight as the back doors swung open.

"Found you some cactus boy," Flash said as he grabbed Jim's ankles and yanked him toward the back of the van. "Get up!"

He did as he was told, blinking in the glare. His eyes adjusted. They were a hundred yards off the highway; on a dirt road that separated an olive orchard from a field of sunflowers. Now out of the mountains, the temperature was back up to 100 degrees and as he turned to his right he saw patches of Opuntia cacti in a ditch. He glanced over his shoulder. Flash was behind him with the Alien pistol in his hand as usual, Boone was passed out in the van, and Billy was in the driver's seat; waiting impatiently for Flash to get this done. Jim took a deep breath and a step down the slope of the ditch.

"You're gonna need to untie me," he said as he turned his head slightly toward Flash.

Flash audibly grumbled and then walked forward. He holstered his gun, took out a blade and cut the tape around Jim's wrists. Jim let his arms dangle freely at his sides for a moment and gave one more quick glance toward Billy who was still behind the wheel, not even looking.

"Hurry up halfbreed, we haven't got all day!" Flash said.

"I'm gonna need some gloves."

Flash laughed out loud. "That's okay, it won't hurt my feelins if you cut yourself up a bit."

"Why don't you just go ahead and cut one off?" Jim asked with his back turned.

"You're the Injun, you do it."

Jim smiled to himself, looked at the cactus and reached his hands forward. He carefully grabbed the bottom of one of the paddle shaped pads and twisted it back and forth until it broke free. One of the many long spikes pierced through the skin of his finger like a sewing needle, but Jim knew that was inevitable. It was like it was covered in barbed wire, with each barb being two inches in length. He repeated that process again and then turned to Flash with two cactus pads, one in each hand and a trickle of blood dripping from his palm.

"Them spines are mighty sharp ain't they Halfbreed," Flash said after a spiteful chuckle and a gappy grin. "That's why they call em Prickly Pears eh?"

"Yeah…yeah they are very sharp," Jim said, looking straight into Flash's bruised up face.

Jim then tossed one of the pads up in the air like a softball, right at Flash's head. As soon as it left his fingers, he charged him with a sudden burst of speed and Flash instinctively put his hands up and ducked to avoid the spiny cactus. Jim tackled him like a linebacker and drove his body into the ground, pinning him on his back. He placed his left hand on Flash's throat and then swung the other cactus pad with his right hand like a tomahawk, pummeling it into Flash's face. He pressed it down hard, crushing and twisting it into his nose, cheek and eye, causing Flash to start shrieking like a cloud of bats escaping a cave.

"At least no one will call you spineless no more!" Jim said before releasing his bloody hand and removing Flash's gun from his holster, just as Billy was frantically emerging from the van and drawing his own pistol. Jim made a dash toward the other side of the vehicle as Billy fired a shot, kicking up an explosion of dust near Jim's feet.

Jim slid to a stop and put his boots against the rear tire, paused and listened. He crouched down and peered underneath the vehicle to get a read on where Billy was standing but he didn't see anything. He turned and looked down both sides of the van, no Billy in sight, and not a sound was heard besides the painful mourns of Flash. Jim turned around and faced the vehicle, bent his knees and leaped upward, placing his hands on the roof of the van and skillfully hoisting himself on top with the pistol still in his grasp. He stayed low and rolled over as the aluminum panelling banged and thumped beneath him.

With all the noise and Jim's location obvious, Billy ran to the back of the van to get an angle on him but in so doing, exposed himself to Jim, who was laying flat on his stomach, with both hands on the Alien. Jim squeezed the trigger, a shot rang out and Billy fell, although it was unclear if he was hit or went down on his own volition. Jim didn't wait to find out. He jumped off the roof and slid into the driver's seat, pulled the lever into reverse, and floored the gas pedal.

Jim backed the van up, parallel to highway 20, shifted into drive and merged onto the road and headed toward Yuba City. He yanked out Boone's phone from his back pocket and noticed that the red dot had continued to move west and was now a good 80 miles or so in front of him.

"How you doin back there Booney?" he yelled as he flew down the highway. "You sleep through all of that?"

There was still no answer from Boone's laid up broken body in the back of the van. "You know that tracker you planted was quite something," he said, realizing at this point he may as well have been talking to himself. He looked again at the Gumshoe application, and prayed that it was indeed Sam moving the red dot along.

He drove down the road a few more miles and Boone's phone started ringing. Jim looked down, the caller ID just said 'Prez'. He picked it up and put it to his ear.

"Hey Booney, we in Marin, gonna book a motel up in Willits for the night, were you at?"

Jim stayed silent for a moment. Just the sound of Snod's voice made his blood boil with the knowledge that he had been responsible for Popeye's death.

"Booney, you there?"

"Boone can't come to the phone right now," Jim said.

There was a long pause on the other end.

"Where's Billy?"

"Billy can't come to the phone either."

"When I get my hands on you Tumbleweed, I'm gonna slaughter you like we slaughtered all your people."

"Not if I find you first."

Sam and Kima pulled into the Pine Cone Motel in Willits, California as the sun was beginning to sink behind the brilliant emerald of the coastal mountains. The ride had been gorgeous and whimsical. Sam knew that under different circumstances she would have been able to appreciate it more, but still, the soft greens and yellows of the countryside had flooded her with emotion and memories that she didn't know she had.

Willits had a lovely ambiance as well. It felt like it was on the edge of the wilderness. Entering the town she noticed a sign that read, 'Gateway to the Redwoods' and taking in the surroundings, she could see why. The whole area was encircled by huge evergreens, and it was quite the welcome change from the barren desert landscape she had grown up in.

They backed up their motorcycles in front of a single story strip of rooms, next to several other bikes already parked. There were people all around outside and as soon as Kima stepped off her Harley, she was greeted by a large man in a black leather cut.

"Glad you made it," the man said as he embraced Kima warmly, before turning toward Sam. "Who's this?"

Kima stretched her legs and took off her glossy, bug splattered dome. "This is Sam, she's been riding with me since Nevada," she said, hanging the helmet over her handlebars. "She needs a place to stay for the night."

The man gave Sam a friendly gaze. He was tall and thin, yet muscular through the chest. He had obsidian hair pulled back and twisted into a single braid that hung nearly to his waist. He was clean shaven, or at least had no facial hair, and his eyes were dark and peaceful. A detailed portrait of Sitting Bull was tattooed on his left arm and a scar ran from his right nostril almost to the bridge of his nose. His vest had the same '13 and half' marking that Kima's had, only his said Redrum, instead of Redspirit.

"Any friend of Kima's is welcome here," he said with a smile.

"Thank you," Sam said as she removed her helmet as well as her bandana.

"They call me Mato," he said, reaching out and shaking her hand.

"Nice to meet you," Sam said, taking a look around and running her fingers through her wind blown hair. The entire parking lot was filled with motorcycles and there were a couple of charcoal grills giving the air a delicious barbecue flavor. There were dozens of men and women, drinking beer and mingling, some banging powwow drums in a circle and chanting, and all wearing matching black cuts. Sam looked back at Mato, focusing on his patches and colors. "What's Redrum?"

He raised his eyebrows with delight. "Redrum is why we're here, we're all Redrum members," he said as he pulled down on his vest. "Kima just joined our sister club, but we all together," he added as he gave Kima a loving pat on the shoulder.

Sam swiveled her boot on the concrete with trepidation. "You sure it's okay for me to be here?"

"Of course, we all just trying to spread positivity, two wheels at a time," Mato said as a smirk formed on his face. "Don't worry it's not murder spelled backwards."

"Oh, no I didn't think that," Sam said with a nervous smile.

Mato let out a rollicking laugh. "Is any word purposefully read backwards anyway?" he asked rhetorically before motioning with his hand. "Come on, you must be exhausted."

Kima grabbed some stuff out of her saddlebags while Sam shoved toiletries in a plastic grocery bag before carrying it to the building just behind where they parked their bikes.

"You two can take this one, key cards inside," Mato said as he opened up a door and made a welcoming gesture with his hands.

They entered into a sterile smelling room which was equipped with a small fridge, a television and a big framed picture of giant redwood trees that hung between two queen-sized beds. They dropped their bags on the ground and Kima sat herself down on the mattress closest to the window, so Sam went over to the other one, tossed her bandana and jacket aside and collapsed onto the springy bed. She placed her hands on her head and let out a huge breath.

Kima took a swig of water and turned toward Sam while still in a sitting position. "What are you going to do?"

Sam peered over at her, as if the question had broken her out of a daze. "I don't know. I suppose I'll leave in the morning."

Kima looked at her for a long time. "You don't want to talk about it do you," she said before taking another sip of water. She leaned against the headboard. "I won't say anything."

Sam smiled. "Thank you. Thank you for everything."

Kima stared at the popcorn ceiling. "Sometimes it's good to have people looking out for you."

Sam twirled her legs over the side of her bed. The sight of Jim's brown leather jacket caused a swing of sadness. Kima saw that she was welling up with tears. She sat down beside her and placed her hand on the bare skin of her shoulder. Not a word was said for several moments. They just sat until Sam got up to get some toilet paper from the bathroom to dry her cheeks and eyes. She plopped back down next to Kima, and sniffling, pulled on the thin straps of her well worn shirt.

"I should throw this thing away."

Kima went and grabbed a black tank top from the small bag next to her bed, and dropped it in Sam's lap.

"It's clean," she said with a shrug. "Just bring it back someday."

Sam cleared her throat and dabbed her cheek again, before placing her hand on the shirt and breaking into a smile, almost a laugh.

"Thanks but I doubt..."

"It's stretchy," Kima said as she wrapped her arm around her and gave her a squeeze before rising to her feet again. "You can have the

169

bathroom if you want, I'm gonna go get some food."

Sam nodded and Kima walked out the door.

Sam stripped herself of her clothes and jumped in the shower. Thoughts of Jim came at her hard as she washed the dust of the road off her sun soaked skin and wind fluttered hair. Her heart felt both light and heavy at the same time. Light with the excitement of newfound love, and heavy with the idea of losing it.

After the shower she dried her hair with the motel provided blower, brushed her teeth, then put on the black shirt. It fit her more like a crop top, not going down far enough to cover her midriff, but knowing the crowd of people she was with, she figured she'd fit right in and she laughed in spite of herself.

Felling better after cleaning up, she threw on her jeans and covered herself in Jim's jacket, as the now darkened sky had finally caused the temperature to dip below 80 degrees, and she headed outside.

Soft Bill Miller music was playing out of some speakers that were set up around the perimeter, and the barbecue grills were still going strong. There was even a Navajo style fry bread stand being run by a few women in Redspirit vests next to a van. After waiting in a couple of short lines, she sat down on a curb that ran along the sidewalk surrounding the motel with a juicy cheeseburger, a powdered sugar topped circle of bubbly fry bread and a bottle of Cosmic Arrow beer. Tired and hungry, the food tasted amazing. She ate with gusto and breathed in the fresh clean air under a starry sky, and started to enjoy the evening in spite of herself. After finishing her burger and forking the last piece of fry bread between her lips, she saw Mato coming her way.

"Good you found somethin to eat," he said as he sat down beside her.

"Yeah, it was so good," she said as she licked some speckles of white sugar off her mouth.

"They always do a good job with this stuff. We'll be here all week if you wanna come back."

She put her empty paper plate down between them and smiled. "Might have to if the food is this delicious."

Mato grinned and then sighed. "Kima says you've been through some stuff."

Sam looked straight ahead and nodded. She noticed that some people were moving one of the egg-shaped grills into the center of the parking lot and filling it with split logs and kindling.

"How long have you known Kima?" Sam asked.

"Not that long actually," he said. "She's kind of new to our family, but she's been pretty enthusiastic."

Sam nodded and played with her fingernails.

"We're doing a prayer ride tomorrow, from here up to Klamath," Mato said as the rest of the group started to gather in a large circle. "You're welcome to join us."

She turned and gave him a halfhearted smile and just said, "thanks."

"Cool," he said, standing up and reaching out his arm. "Time to pay our respects, come on."

She grabbed his hand and rose to her feet. She had been wondering where Kima was, and then saw that she was standing in the middle of the parking lot, with a microphone in her hand, next to the egg shaped barbecue pot that was now blazing with fire. Everyone was joining hands and surrounding her, so Sam followed suit. The music in the background quieted but still played as the people bowed their heads and gave their full attention to Kima, who brought the microphone to her mouth and began delivering a kind of prayer.

"Miles will never distance the depth of respect between us, as sisters and brothers of the spirit wind. As you close your eyes, smile my friend, think of the many miles still left to ride. Hold onto memories, never give up on life, for as long as I breathe, you are a part of me, as long as I ride you shall ride with me and when I leave here to join you there, others will ride for us," Kima said, her voice loud and clear and echoing into the night. When she continued, everyone joined her in unison. "ONWARD FOREVER FORWARD INTO THE WIND, TO THE WIND, ONCE MORE TO THE WIND."

Just as they closed for a moment of silence, a thundering rumble took over the spiritual atmosphere. All attention was drawn toward the street where dozens of Harleys were turning into the Skunk Train Motel, directly across from the Pine Cone. Even in the darkness of night it was evident that all of the riders were wearing matching black cuts, brodies and stahlhelms, and Sam lifted her toes to get a better look at their colors. Sure enough, silver and black letters spelling out, Iron Raiders.

Dice Moya stood at the front desk of the Skunk Train Motel and listened to the guy explain the situation again.

"I'm sorry we have a policy not to let y'all stay here on account of what happened last time," said the desk clerk, a nervous overweight man in his early 20s.

"We called ahead and already reserved it," Dice said as he pointed his finger on the counter and glared at him.

"I'm sorry that was a mistake," the clerk said. Beads of perspiration were visible from his prematurely receding hairline and dripping down his forehead.

There was a loud thud, and both men turned their heads to see that Snod Farkus had just kicked open the door to the small lobby.

"What's takin so long?" Snod snarled in a hissing spew as he trudged forward, his massive lumbering frame shaking the entire room.

"He sayin they won't take us," Dice said. He leaned against the counter like he didn't have a care in the world, his golden hoop earrings glistening in the overhead lights.

Snod pounded his fist on the desk like a Viking and stuck his greasy messy mustache right into the young motel worker's face.

"We gonna need at least twelve rooms!" Spit and drool flew from his face as he spoke. "More if you got it."

The young clerk was sweating harder now and he looked so scared and nervous that Dice wondered if he was going to pass out.

"I'm sorry," the clerk said in a terrified snivel. Snod grabbed him by the collar of his ill fitting navy blue polo shirt, twisted his fist hard, whipped out his knife with his other hand and brushed it against his nostril.

"Give us the rooms now!" Snod said. "Or you can pay it through the nose."

"Is there a problem here?"

Everyone spun around and saw that the sheriff had just walked through the door. He was less than middle aged, tall and well built. His khaki shirt was held together by silver buttons and he wore a big cowboy hat atop his crew cut head.

"We just want our rooms," Snod said.

The sheriff looked at him, and then made his way over to the clerk.

"Thank God you're here," the clerk said.

The sheriff gave Snod another quick glance. Snod turned his hip to showcase his holstered Ruger.

The sheriff put his arm on the young clerk's shoulder and took him aside. "Listen, um, you have enough rooms available?"

"Uh, yeah but...we have a policy..." the clerk whimpered.

"I'm going to need you to go ahead and give em the rooms," the sheriff said. He seemed almost as nervous as the clerk. He saw that these men were Iron Raiders, and he was well aware of

174

their reputation. "We don't, we don't want any trouble."

"What?" the clerk asked in disbelief.

"Just do it!" the sheriff shouted as he turned away. He looked over at Snod and lowered the brim of his hat to show respect. "Sorry fellas, y'all have yourself a nice night tonight."

Snod cleared his throat long and hard and then spat a thick lump of brown saliva on the sheriff's black boots.

"You bet your buttons we will," he said.

#

Jim Deere exited Highway 101 and rolled into Willits in the darkness of night. He could see from the tracker exactly where his Indian Scout was located, but he still had Boone in the back, and he needed to be dealt with.

He turned off the main street onto a side road in a quiet neighborhood and pulled over. He grabbed the pen that was standing up in the cup holder of the center console, stepped out of the van and went back in through the rear. Crouching next to Boone, he lightly slapped his face.

"Wake up," he said as Boone gradually opened his eyes and groaned in discomfort. "Come on, you're okay."

Boone turned his neck and blinked several times. "Huhh, uh, where…who are you?"

Jim put his hand on his forehead, he was feverish, wet with sweat and his skin was grey.

"How's the leg?"

"Tumbleweed? Where…where am I?"

"I need to get you to a hospital, but gotta take off this splint first."

Jim loosened the bungee cord and the tape that was holding the Winchester to his leg.

"Does that hurt?" he asked, noticing that Boone's face was not reacting to the movement.

He peered down at the knee, it looked and smelled horrible.

"I don't wanna die."

"Good," Jim said as he continued to unravel the medical tape.

"Did we uh, find the treasure?" Boone asked as his face formed a slight smile of delirium.

"The treasure don't belong to you."

"I'm sorry." Boone's eyes turned suddenly soft and kind, in a way that Jim had never seen before. "I'm sorry about everything, this was all Snod's idea."

"I know."

He freed the rifle and hid it underneath a blanket. He then removed all of Boone's effects, his switchblade and wallet. He tore off the back cover of the van's owner's manual from the sleeve behind the middle seat and looked at Boone's cell phone, wrote down Snod's number, folded the paper and shoved it into Boone's pocket. Wherever Snod was, he knew he was likely close by, and Boone, Jim thought, might be a perfect distraction to slow him and the Iron Raiders down.

Back in the driver's seat he cruised onto main street and turned toward the Wounded Knee Memorial hospital that he had passed on the way in. He put the van in the far end of the poorly lit parking lot, groomed his hair with his hands and stepped out. He jogged to the main entrance, stopped, and peered inside. There was a front desk receptionist in the middle of a t-shaped hallway that veered out to either side. He drew a quick breath, stood up straight and walked in.

The woman behind the desk smiled at him and he smiled back but kept on walking like he had been there a hundred times before. He took a right down the shiny linoleum floored hall and stuck his head in a few doorways and waiting areas as he strolled by, until he found an unattended stretcher in an unoccupied unlit room. He grabbed it without hesitation and wheeled it out an exit on the side of the building and didn't look back. He pushed it into the parking lot and returned to the van.

"Time to go buddy," he said after opening the back doors. He held on to Boone's good leg and pulled. "This is gonna be intense."

Jim yanked on his body and after some struggle, flopped him onto the stretcher, while Boone moaned in annoyance.

Jim slammed the doors shut and pushed him through the parking lot at a brisk pace. When he reached the main entrance he slowed, and just when he got close enough for the automatic doors to spread open he gave Boone one final shove, turned around and ran back to the van.

The stretcher rolled through the lobby of the hospital and gently bumped into the front desk and the receptionist jolted her head up in attention.

"I knew they would be coming this way, but I didn't think they would be right across the street," Sam said from the confines of her motel room. She sat on the edge of her mattress and ran her hands over the sides of her head as she spoke. "I don't know, they've found me three times already, somehow they just know everything!"

Kima walked over and sat beside her. "Your father wanted you to have his treasure, but they found out, and now they're after it, right?"

"They killed him to get to it!"

"We've got history with them too."

"I need to find it before they do, they have the map."

"And so do you?" Kima asked, confused.

Sam bit her lip. "I took a picture."

Kima sighed. "You're not gonna find anything in the middle of the night."

"It's not even the treasure at this point, I just want to find Jim."

"And you know they have him?"

Sam stood up and ran her fingers through her hair again. "I'm sure they do," she said with a sinking voice. "He still won't answer his phone, but I know he'll find a way to stay alive."

"We should wait before we do anything, you look so tired."

Sam paced back and forth in front of the bed for a few moments, then Kima sprang to her feet.

"You said they found you three times already?"

Sam stopped. "Yeah."

Kima's eyes widened. She grabbed Sam's arm. "Come outside with me."

Sam followed her out the door and into the parking lot. Kima went immediately to Jim's motorcycle and began studying it with intense focus. She ran her fingers under the front fender and then kneeled down beside it and did the same thing to the back.

"What are you doing?" Sam asked.

Kima struggled to contort her hand deep into the nooks and crannies above the back tire. She grabbed something, twisted and pulled hard. Finally she turned to Sam with a small plastic device in her hand.

"This is why they found you."

Sam's eyes sharpened. "What is that?" She stepped forward to get a closer look.

Kima pinched it between her thumb and index finger and walked a few paces until she was under one of the outdoor lamp posts. "It's a homing device, someone planted this."

Sam studied it, and then turned to Kima in horror. "So they do know where we are!"

"We need to get rid of this, right now," Kima said, lowering her voice.

"Where?"

Kima turned her head toward the Skunk Train Motel. "Back where it came from."

Jim drove by the Skunk Train, looked at Boone's phone, then stopped the van. He peered out the window again. The entire parking lot of the motel was filled with motorcycles, most of them Harleys as far as he could tell. He backed up and made a u-turn and parked on the same side road he had been on earlier.

He walked toward the motel and checked the phone again. He could have sworn that the red dot had been on the other side of the street when he had driven by the first time. To his left was the dimly lit sign of The Pine Cone Motel, and to his right was the bright neon of The Skunk Train, both parking lots crammed with bikes.

He slunk to the right, which was where the map was leading but he stopped and ducked down when he saw two figures emerge from one of the rooms. He recognized the shaved head and gold hoop earrings of Dice Moya as well as the flaming hair and gigantic build of Red Dog O'Manbun.

He hid behind a snowberry bush at the base of a sycamore, between the sidewalk and the motel and watched. According to the phone, his Indian had to be in the parking lot ahead, hidden amongst the Harleys. He could hear the two men talking.

"I don't see nothin," Red Dog said.

"There were two a them, I swear," Dice said.

Jim gazed in the direction that the men were looking, across the street. He waited a while behind the bush until they went back to their rooms and then made his way to the Pine Cone. He searched briefly through the darkness at all the motorcycles in the lot. They too were mostly Harleys, although he did notice a few Japanese bikes as well, and even a couple Moto Guzzis, indicating the place was not occupied by the Iron Raiders.

He went inside the office, confused. By now it was getting late, and the room was empty aside from a man feeding dollar bills into a soda machine in the corner off to his left. There was no one at the front desk. He approached the counter and pressed down on the shiny metal bell, making a high pitched ringing noise. Several moments later a woman appeared.

"Yes?"

"Hi, just wondering if I could get a room for the night," Jim said, as the guy to his left started banging on the soda machine.

"You see the sign?" the woman asked with a huff. "No vacancy."

Jim's eyes lowered to the carpet. He was so tired that his neck was having trouble supporting his own head. "Oh, okay." He turned to leave.

"Hey," a voice said.

Jim whirled around to see it was the soda guy. He was tall, had long black hair braided into a ponytail, and a scar on his nose.

"Yeah?"

The man sneered at him. "What are you doin here?"

"Just lookin for a room."

The man stepped forward with his can of orange pop. "Not here you're not, go back to your own side."

"What do you mean?"

"I mean this," the man said as he grabbed Jim's forearm and pointed at his tattoo. "What are people doing here anyway?"

"I ain't one of them," Jim said before clearing his throat. "No more."

The guy's eyes went from Jim's arm and then to his face. He stared hard and tightened his brow. "You're first nations ain't ya?"

Jim glared back, trying not to look too long at his nose. "Half."

"What you mean no more? Nobody leaves the Iron Raiders."

Jim shook free of the man's grip and stood tall. "No one except me."

He turned away, went out the door, walked back across the street and surveyed the parking lot of the Skunk Train again, all seemed quiet. Nothing could make the Iron Raiders sleep like a long hot day on the road, although he thought sooner or later, Snod would be receiving a call from a local hospital.

Jim took out the phone and followed it through the clutter of Harleys to the exact location indicated by the red dot. A motorcycle sat parked right in front of him, but it was not his, It was Snod Farkus's Road King. He looked around, no sign of his Scout at all.

He thought he heard a noise coming from the motel. He was so tired he wondered if he was seeing or even thinking clearly. He had not slept well the night before to put it mildly, and he walked away, trudging down the street, bewildered. When he reached the van, he crawled in through the back, collapsed and draped himself in the blanket next to the Winchester. He ate a packaged concha. Thoughts of Sam being somewhere out there tormented him, but before he could think of what to do about it, he was asleep.

*"Are you all right?*
*is there something you want to say?*
*are you all right?*
*just tell me that you're OK."*

Sam Diego woke up early the next morning with the first sign of light beaming through the thin translucent drapes of the motel window. When she went to the bathroom she realized she had been so tired, she had fallen asleep in Kima's shirt, which was good she thought, as it was easier to get ready that way. She tied back her hair and put her bandana on, anxious for the day ahead. Her entire body was pulsing with nervous energy, so much so that it wasn't until she went to grab her plastic grocery bag of belongings that she saw she was alone, and then, as if right on cue, the door opened.

It was Kima. "Good morning," she said, handing her a steaming hot styrofoam cup of coffee and a blueberry muffin from the complementary continental breakfast. "I talked to Mato, hope you don't mind but the ruckus across the street really started up some conversation. I told him about Jim, says he met a boy last night that seemed to fit his description, at least the way he put it to me."

Sam nearly dropped the coffee on the carpet. "Where is he?"

"Outside."

Sam blinked. "Jim?"

Kima froze for a second. "No no, sorry Mato is just right out there," she said, gesturing at the window. "Go to him, ask him."

Sam gasped, spun around, and then bolted out the door. She turned to the right and saw Mato sitting next to an ashtray at the edge of the parking lot in front of his room. She scurried toward him, losing a few splashes of coffee in the process.

"What happened?" she asked, seating herself in the vacant white plastic chair beside him.

Mato sat up after a puff on his cigarillo. He cleared his throat. "Kima, she told me about how you were riding with another guy, hadn't thought to put it together."

"Did you see him?" Sam asked as she scooted herself closer.

Mato had a serious look on his face. "All I know is this guy tried to get a room last night." He took another slow drag from his smoke. "This place was full anyway, but I recognized his tattoo and sort of kicked him out, how could I know?"

Sam's shoulders slumped and her eyes lowered. "What did he look like?"

"Young guy, part native I think."

She paused for a moment, letting the steam of the coffee rise beneath her chin. "Was he handsome?"

Mato twirled his head and gazed at her, expressionless. "Looked beat up, could barely keep his eyes open. You wanna tell me what's goin on?"

186

She crossed her legs and let out a short pant. "They killed my father. They're after something that belongs to me," she said as she looked at the Skunk Train Motel, its parking lot still full of motorcycles. She turned back to Mato. "Where did he go…afterwards?"

"Don't know, went across the street I think."

"He was walking free last night," she said, befuddled. "I don't know where to look for him other than to…where I'm going."

Mato puffed one more time on his cigarillo before stabbing it out in the ashtray to his right. He gave Sam a long and heavy stare. "You better get going then."

Snod Farkus was snoring like a chainsaw, his freely tumbling brown hair falling in mysterious waves over drool stained pillows. when a loud ringing noise jared him from a delightful dream. He opened his eyes and flopped his hand around on the nightstand, searching for his phone. After a few failed attempts in locating it, he sat up and realized the ringing was coming from the bed, hidden beneath the blankets. He grabbed it but before he could answer, his neck and head convulsed in a thunderous sneeze, and after wiping the chartreuse green snot off his mustache, he put the phone to his ear, and caressed his bloated stomach.

"Hello?"

The sound of his voice caused Dice Moya to sit up in the other bed. Charles Bukowski, or Meatbone, began stirring from his spot on the floor.

"Yes this is Snod Farkus."

Dice noticed that a look of terror had come across Snod's face.

"Mmhmm, yes, yeah, yeah," Snod said with a few somber nods. "Will he be okay?"

His eyes went wide, and then the phone fell from his hand.

"What?" asked Dice, leaning forward.

Snod turned. "Boone's in the hospital."

Dice's face was overcome with shock. "What hospital?"

"Here," Snod said. "The hospital here in town!"

Dice sprang to his feet without a second of hesitation and began pulling his camouflage pants over his bare legs. "Let's go see him, one of us gets cut, we all bleed."

"Wait," Snod said in a whisper.

Dice stopped with his pants still halfway up his thick, hairy thighs. "What?"

Snod's eyebrows were raised and his mouth was agape. "If Boone is here," he said, raising his index finger in the air as if to show that his brain was thinking. "That means Tumbleweed is here too."

Dice's eyes darted from right to left and then back again. "So, if we see em, we capture em."

"Right," Snod said. He then pointed his finger toward the floor at Meatbone. "You stay here, keep an eye out just in case, tell Red Dog to stay with you." He then moved his finger to Dice. "You get everybody up, we're goin to Wounded Knee Memorial."

Jim Deere watched from the branches of an old sycamore tree as the Iron Raiders pulled out of the Skunk Train parking lot and rode away. He looked down, all of the motorcycles were gone with the exception of two. He hopped from limb to limb with the Winchester in his right hand as he made his way to the lawn at ground level.

He ran toward the remaining bikes, and turned in the direction of the motel.

"Sam!" he yelled. He took a few steps closer, wary that they may be watching him. "Sam!" he yelled again. He was standing too far out in the open, too exposed and he knew it. Then, in the corner of his eye he saw Meatbone and his short thick mohawk atop his bulbous head, charging at him like a raging bull. He turned to run, only to see that Reg Dog was on the other side of him, blocking his obvious exit to the sidewalk. He took a few quick steps to his left and dove into the snowberry bush, causing Meatbone and Red Dog to nearly collide with each other.

Jim rolled onto his back still with the rifle in hand. As he tried to get up and make a run for it, the blue morning sky above him was suddenly blocked out by the flaming hair and body of Red Dog soaring through the air like a flying squirrel.

He landed on top of him and instantly sunk his stubby fingers into Jim's flesh like chicken claws.

Still lying on his back, Jim dug his boots into the dirt and slid himself backward before jerking his leg up and kneeing Red Dog in the chin, sandwiching his outstretched tongue between brittle yellow teeth with a solid wet crunch. Jim rolled Red Dog's 250 plus pound body off and vaulted to his feet as Meatbone was closing in.

Meatbone's upper lip was drawn high like it was being sucked up by his flaring nostrils and Jim spun the Winchester backward in the nick of time so that the curved end of the stock caught him square in the neck. He went down with a gurgling thud and Jim jumped over him as Red Dog struggled to get back to his feet.

Jim ran through the bush, back into the parking lot and toward the sidewalk but before he could make it to the street he was blocked by a motorcycle that came screeching to halt, seemingly out of nowhere. He looked. It wasn't a Harley. It was an Indian Scout, and the person riding it was Sam.

"Get on," she yelled over the revving engine.

Jim stood still for a moment, he was having trouble believing what his eyes were seeing. On the back of Sam's tiny black shirt there was, spelled out in bold pink letters, a phrase that said: 'If you can read this the jerk fell off'. He heard swearing and grumbling and glanced to his right. Red Dog and Meatbone were stampeding toward them like a pair of rabid wolves. He turned back to Sam, confronted with a decision.

He lunged forward and tossed his leg over the seat behind her. Still with the rifle in his grasp and the Alien pistol stuffed in his tight jeans, he straddled his thighs against her hips and she kicked the bike into gear and took off with a lurch.

Jim looked back as Sam accelerated down main street and saw that the two men behind them had already jumped on their Harleys. Sam shifted up into third and then fourth gear, blowing through a stop sign and splitting passed cars at well over 50 miles per hour.

"Put your helmet on!" she yelled as she prepared to merge onto the 101.

"Ok," Jim shouted as he slid the rifle beneath his knees and unhooked the helmet from the backrest behind him. He managed to strap it on securely just as Sam blasted onto the highway and opened up the throttle. He looked back. Red Dog and Meatbone were hot on their trail, only about a hundred yards away. He turned forward and saw a state trooper SUV headed toward them, going the opposite direction.

"Cop," he shouted as Sam shifted down and took her hand off the gas.

"I see em," she said.

Jim moved his legs in an effort to hide the rifle the best he could and crossed his fingers. After they flew by each other he twisted around to see that the police car was still rushing south with no signs of slowing down. Sam was looking in the rear view mirror and Jim found himself instinctively wrapping his arms around her waist as he felt the bike increasing in speed once again.

The highway narrowed into two lanes as they entered a landscape of rolling hills covered in a dense old growth forest and the Harley Softail was gaining on them fast. Jim's heart felt ready to beat out of his chest when he looked back and saw that Red Dog had pulled a pistol out with his left hand. Jim covered Sam's helmet with his palm and out of impulse yelled in her ear.

"Swerve!"

The bike leaned and shook to the left as two single-action shots rang out. Jim closed his eyes for a second but felt nothing and Sam increased her speed to over 100 miles per hour. Jim jolted upward with his feet on the back floorboards and kicked his right leg over to the left side while holding the rifle in the air. He curled himself back and swiveled his butt on the seat until he was straddling the sissy bars and facing the opposite direction.

Without a qualm he yanked down the lever and pointed the Winchester directly at the front tire of the Softail and pulled the trigger.

The bike's back wheel immediately shot upward and Red Dog was thrown into the air like a crash test dummy. Meatbone narrowly missed colliding with the flipped over wreckage but he kept going and actually proceeded to close the gap. Sam leaned into a turn and Jim nearly lost his balance as he attempted to aim the rifle again. Regrouping as Meatbone loomed, Jim closed one eye and lined up his sight. He pulled the trigger but this time all he heard was a clicking sound. The rifle was empty.

There was a dreadful sense of panic as Jim saw Meatbone trying the same maneuver, pulling out a gun with his left while his right stayed heavy on the throttle. He was close, much closer than Red Dog had been when he had tried this, only 15 yards back, coming up on them along Sam's right and Jim's left, as he was still facing backward. Jim twisted his neck around and yelled as loud as he could at Sam. "Let go of your right hand!"

Sam understood and released her grip from the throttle and the motorcycle decelerated. The distance between Jim and Meatbone disappeared like they were connected by a magnetic force and they were side by side in an instant. Jim looked down and held tight to the rifle's stock. Meatbone pointed the gun at Jim's chest at near point blank range. Jim caught a glimpse of the silver spokes of the Harley glistening in the sunlight and that was all he needed. He thrust the barrel of the gun straight into the front wheel like a spear and let go before contact while Sam leaned into another turn. Meatbone's bike exploded over the side railing of the road, flipping and rotating over itself twice and then rapidly diminishing in size as Jim and Sam pulled away at a speed nearing triple digits.

They continued north on the 101 for a few more miles before Sam pulled over onto a gravel clearing at the edge of a redwood forest. She stepped off the bike and removed her helmet in a rapture of excitement and disbelief. Jim's heart was still racing, yet he also felt an eruption of relief and joy that she was there with him. He dismounted, placed his hands on his knees and peering up at her, asked, "Are you okay?"

"Am I okay?" she said, speaking animatedly with her hands. "Are you okay?"

Jim unsnapped his helmet and she fell into his arms. They squeezed each other tight, neither one of them wanting to let go, both of them in a surreal state of shock. Jim put his hands on her shoulders and looked at her face to face.

"Where did you learn to ride like that?"

She smiled at him for a moment, then drew her gaze up at the highway above. Her eyes still big as saucers. "People had to have seen us."

He sighed. "They were tracking us."

Her look went toward the ground. "I know, don't worry it's gone now, but we should keep going."

He was a little confused but he nodded. "You know where?"

She raised her eyebrows up and down, then turned away, put her helmet back on and got on the bike. "Let's go," she said. "Cops will be comin around soon, and who knows about the rest of them."

Jim couldn't help but smile as he jumped on the seat behind her and watched her kick it into gear.

They cruised north for about an hour, this time at a law-abiding speed. They stopped briefly in the woodsy town of Garberville to fill the gas tank, get water and check the map. Jim handled the pump, she ran inside, and they were out of there in no time at all.

Back on the 101 they continued north past Myers Flat, with Sam still gripping the black anodized finish of the handlebars. It seemed that with every mile they traveled, the bigger the trees were getting. After streaming passed a sign that said 'Humboldt Redwoods State Park' there was a poorly marked road cutting west through the giant forest and, following the direction of the map, they took it, both feeling much safer once they were off the highway and away from the eyes of others.

The road was nothing more than a slender strip of asphalt, so remote and lightly trafficked that it didn't even necessitate a yellow center line. Enormous ancient redwoods towered over them in all directions and blocked out the sun and sealed them in like a comforting swathe. It was all Sam could do to keep her eyes on the winding pavement and not look up and be awed by their splendor.

After around ten miles of traveling at roughly 30 miles per hour, weaving through the biggest trees they had ever seen, the bumpy asphalt turned to gravel, and the road lifted upward.

Sam curved slowly through the hills, staying mostly in second and third gear for miles at a time. The road traversed back and forth, bent so tightly with hairpin turn after hairpin turn. It was exhausting and nauseating work, but the country and wilderness that surrounded them was nothing short of spectacular. About 40 minutes into their plodding and rugged meandering of potholes, loose gravel, and dramatic inclines, Sam pulled the bike over and killed the engine.

She stepped off and unsnapped her helmet. "I just need a break, this is too much," she said in a breathy voice.

Suddenly she started giggling as she bent over and placed her hands on her knees. She continued giggling for long enough that it became infectious to the point where they were both laughing uncontrollably, just at themselves and the absurdity of everything, the road just being the metaphorical straw that broke the back.

"Oh, oh man, I'm sorry, this is all just too much!" she said, trying to compose herself amid outbursts of intractable hilarity. She let herself collapse into him and he held her for a long time as the soft quivering and vibrations of their laughter and furor eventually dwindled into something between deranged bliss and sanity. Once she caught her breath she stepped back and stretched her legs on her tippy toes, lifting her arms into an arch over her head, causing her tiny top to ride even higher above her exposed belly button, showcasing the silky smooth skin of her waist.

"Be hard for anyone to find us out here," Jim said as he looked up at the trees. He turned to

Sam, and he found was unable to stop smiling. "How did you…what happened?"

She caught his gaze and saw him nodding at the bike. "I taught myself, didn't think I had a choice." She took a deep breath and leaned against the seat. "What happened to you?"

Jim took his helmet off and scratched his head. "A lot."

"I ran into that woman again," she said after a pause. "The one you helped, I rode with her."

"Redspirit?"

"Yep."

He straightened his body and took a step forward. "You were at the Pine Cone last night then, I met a guy…Redrum."

"Yeah, I talked to him too, started to put it together this morning, it was a Redrum rally, or whatever you call it," she said. "They took your phone?"

"Yeah, but I took theirs." He squinted at her through the rays of sunlight that were beaming between the trees. "That's how I found you, or, maybe how you found me."

She nodded. "The woman, her name's Kima, she figured it out." She turned around and pointed at the rear fender of the bike. "There was like a thing hidden up in here."

"You put it on a Harley across the street?"

She spun toward him. "How did you know?"

"I was just trying to find you."

Her eyes narrowed. "Is the tracker thing still on that bike?"

"Yeah, it was, I was just so out of it last night," he said as he looked at the ground and took a deep breath. "The bike you put it on belong's to Snod Furkus."

She swallowed. "The guy who killed my father?"

Jim nodded.

"That phone is still hooked up to it?" she asked.

"Should be," he said as he searched his pockets and pulled it out. He studied the screen. "They've left the hospital, says he's just north of Willits now. I'm sure they're coming here."

"And now we'll know exactly when." She paused and bit her lip. "Did you say hospital?"

"I'll tell you about it later."

She looked at him with tenderness, and her eyes softened as she languidly pressed her body into him.

"I was so scared," she said, plunging completely into his arms. "This has been insane."

"Yeah, was scared too, I'm so sorry."

"Don't apologize."

There was a moment of introspective silence, to delay the inevitable. He stepped back enough to look at her fully and opened and closed his mouth several times before he spoke. "Is this... something you want to do yourself?"

Her dreamy gaze sharpened. "No." She ran her fingers through the ends of her hair and gave him a subtle yet haughty smirk. "I might need somebody to dig a hole, plus this is your bike."

He grinned. "Then we should go."

"Okay but you can drive, my hands hurt and I'm sick of this road."

Jim Deere fired up the engine, held onto the handlebars and Sam Diego held on to him as they headed down the hill into the valley. The ocean was getting close, they could smell it in the air, then, out of nowhere, there was a small village.

It was the town of Honeydew, although it was hardly a town, just a few Spanish colonial style homes surrounded by cute little farms. The place wasn't even big enough to have a gas station, only a small country store next to a post office. Jim slowed down, squeezed the brake, and put his foot on the ground.

"Should we stop?"

Sam placed her hands on his shoulders. "Need something?"

"Don't know, do we need a shovel?"

She glanced at the store. From the outside it looked like nothing more than a house with a wrap around porch, and no one was parked out front. "Yeah," she said.

They stepped off the bike, removed their helmets and went inside.

It was quaint and charming with a low white ceiling and hardwood floors covered by aisles of basic grocery items as well as a section dedicated to clothing that catered toward tourists and the yoga crowd as well as camping and hiking gear. There was a deli that served both cold and hot sandwiches and an old-fashioned soda jerk. The whole place seemed somehow way nicer than it should be.

A man of wearing a light brown cowboy hat stood behind the counter. He was older, and the wrinkles around his mouth were partially hidden beneath a still black, pencil mustache that outlined his upper lip. "Can I help you folks find anything?" he asked in a subtle yet distinctive paisano accent.

Jim and Sam looked at each other, and then Sam turned to the man. "Do you have any um… gardening supplies?"

The man shrugged and stepped forward. "Sure do," he said as he walked toward them and led them to a back wall. "Gardening and riding a motorcycle, that's something you don't see very often. What brings you to the Lost Coast?"

Jim surveyed the small display of shovels, spades and rakes. Sam turned back to the old man.

"It's beautiful here," she said.

He smiled. "Most beautiful place in the world."

"You get many customers this far out?" Jim asked as he continued to scour the merchandise.

"People live here you know," the man said. "Raise cattle, horses…tourists and hikers come in droves on the weekends."

"We'll take this one," Jim said as he picked out a four foot clam shovel. "And we should get going."

The man nodded and walked them back to the front.

"You must be hungry and thirsty, riding all the way out here," he said as he slid behind the register next to the delicatessen. "Can't let you leave without having a sandwich."

An old woman emerged from the other side of the refrigerated display case. Bacon was frying on an iron panini press in the back, and the smell was more than tempting. Sam looked over at Jim and Jim, although  famished, turned to the old man ready to decline his offer, thinking they didn't have the time, but Sam surprised him.

"I could eat," she said, peering up at a dark green menu board with white chalk written on it. "Avocado BLT sounds amazing, I will have that."

Jim's mouth was watering. "Okay then, I'll take those two things and a cup of coffee." He pointed at the cherry malasadas, sprinkled with sugar and showcased beneath a clear cake tray on the counter.

The old woman glared at Jim while he took out some cash of his wallet.

"I'll try the California Peach soda as well," Sam said.

"Good choice," the old man said as his bushy grey eyebrows slanted tenderly.

The old woman was still staring at Jim. "You look familiar to me," she said.

He drew his eyes in her direction. Her skin was brown and her hair was a silvery grey although it was mostly covered by an aqua blue bonnet. She was frowning, and her dark eyes were steadfast, yet they were surrounded by circles of sadness, as if she had been carrying the weight of the cross on her back for years. "You must have me confused with someone else," Jim said.

She stared at him for another long moment before she turned around to prepare the food.

Sam took her soda in a glass and she and Jim headed out to the front porch where there were tables and chairs. Jim took a huge bite of one of his warm and gooey malasadas, and Sam undid her bandana and let her hair fall. The old man came out a few minutes later and served Jim his coffee and Sam her BLT. They ate in silence for a minute or two, taking in the landscape.

It was a very pleasant 80 degrees and the sun was shining while western meadowlarks sang over the sound of the gentle river in the background. There were a few small gardens and a weathered white picket fence holding in a sparse herd of Merino sheep on the other side of the dirt road. The little farms and houses were whimsical and serene, dotted with wildflowers and pleasing to the eye. The town was surrounded by the mountains and wilderness of the King Range on all sides, serving as a reminder that despite the cuteness, this was the most undeveloped stretch of coastal land in all of California.

"Don't look at me like that," Sam said after she devoured almost half of her sandwich. "We've been going for hours."

"I was just thinkin what if they all come riding through here and ask questions." Jim said in a whisper after taking a sip of his coffee. "I don't want these people to get hurt."

"You still need to eat," she said. "I don't know, where are they now?"

Jim was already looking at the phone. "Same spot."

"That's weird," she said before taking another bite.

"Yeah and this thing is about to run out of batteries."

Ignoring his comment, she finished chewing and said, "Mmm, this is like the best sandwich I have ever had."

"We need to hurry."

She held the remaining third of the BLT in her hands, and saw that Jim had already devoured his pastries. "Then help me finish."

Jim's fears seemed to languish. The spell of Sam's alluring spirit and the smells, sights and sounds that encased him were overwhelming. Her essence entered into him, dreamy and languorous, weakening the fibers of resolution, suffusing the face of mortality or of judgement, with fragrant pines and blossoms mixed with the salty ocean and rays of sun beaming against her soft hair, magnifying the stark contrast of her dark eyes. He looked at her as if he was unsure if she was serious, but he leaned in and she brought the still warm food to his mouth, placing a corner between his teeth. The buttery toast was golden and fluffy and crunchy at the same time. He chewed and savored the taste as well as the sense of normalcy it brought him, if only for an instant. "You're right that is good," he said with his mouth still slightly full.

"If you want more you can get your own," she said as she batted her eyes at him and smiled.

He delighted and indulged in her gaze, until reality hit him and his face became serious.

"You want to talk about, um," he started to say before trailing off, searching for the words. "What happened on the highway?"

"No, not yet. Maybe something to tell my grandkids someday, if I ever have any grandkids."

He took a drink from his coffee and then set it down on the blue painted wooden table. "These people, the Iron Raiders will, uh," he said, again seeking out how to articulate his thoughts. "They'll kill for money."

She swallowed and looked straight at him. She rolled her eyes. "I know."

They crossed the Mattole River on a picturesque one lane bridge and went on riding and twisting their way through the countryside and unfettered forest. With the shovel bungeed behind the backrest, Sam kept an eye on the map from her seat on the back of the bike, and when the road came upon a small summit atop a thickly forested hill, she squeezed Jim's shoulders and said, "Stop."

Jim looked around, he could smell that the ocean was close. They were high up, with the valley behind them and to the left of the road, a private drive overgrown with blackberry and salmonberry bushes, purple foxgloves and brilliant green ferns. "Here?" he asked.

"I think so," she said as she noticed a no trespassing sign that was nailed to a coastal fir.

"Okay."

He clunked down into first gear and rumbled forward. They wound through the path for almost a mile. The road was so unmaintained that the overabundant plant life was actually brushing against them as they plowed through. Finally, they descended into a clearing of the trees and their eyes were bombarded with the magnificent sight of the sea.

"Wait," Sam said, tapping Jim's shoulder and pointing to the right. There was a grassy meadow rounding over a hill where a huge red manzanita tree stood like a flame, majestically alone with seemingly only the deep blue of the Pacific behind it. "I remember this place."

He veered off the road and parked the bike, facing slightly uphill on the flattest ground he could find. In the distance to the left, where the path continued, there was the outline of a house with a brick wall around it and to the right, the silhouette of a split wood fence encasing a sparkling green field.

"Wow," Jim said under his breath as he took in the incredible panoramic view of the charmed setting and jagged coastline in the near distance. He felt as if he were inside a computer's screensaver display image.

Sam stepped onto the ground and inhaled deeply through her nose, relishing the sweet smells and clean air. "This is amazing," she said, holding her arms out at her sides and closing her eyes.

When she opened them again she gazed down at the unusually large manzanita at the edge of the hill. It looked out of place, like something that belonged not in California but somewhere deep in an African savanna. "That's it," she said.

"What?"

She glanced at Jim, flashing a joyous smile. "The wishing tree."

They took their helmets off, hung them on the handlebars and Jim untied the shovel. They began walking toward the tree and he, with the shovel in his left hand, found that his right had slipped into her fingers.

There was a small stream running down the hill that split its way between the house to their left and the fenced in pasture. The creek sang a soothing trickle as water clear as crystal danced over rounded granite and basalt. They crossed it with a skip and a hop and continued down the grassy glade. The sunlight reflected off the manzanita's brightly colored bark which made it appear to glow and gave it an almost ethereal quality. Once there, Sam ran her fingers along its smooth thick trunk.

"This is where I buried my wish," she said.

"So what was your wish?" Jim asked as he stabbed the shovel into the soft turf.

She gazed at him and almost laughed. "I don't remember."

"Let's find out."

Sam circled around the tree. She looked up at the branches, shielding the sun from her eyes with her hand. She turned to the right and studied the earth.

"Do you remember that house?" he asked.

"No, I don't think it was there before."

He blinked and took in the marvelous whimsy of it all. "Strange."

She paced a few steps back from the base of the tree and stopped upon a piece of rhyolite that was jutting up out of the grass like a giant football. She cleared off some dirt to the left of the rock, facing the manzanita directly.

"Here," she said.

Jim looked at her with curious anticipation, walked over and began piercing the ground with the shovel. After flinging away the top layer of grass and dandelions, he braced his boots firmly in the dirt and dug with vigor, gripping the wooden handle tight with both hands.

After several minutes he was more than a foot deep and he was breathing hard. Sam sat perched on the sloping grass with her legs together and her hands upon her knees. The veins in his tan forearms and triceps were bulging and contracting with each savage swing and pitch of the shovel.

The sun beat down and she rolled her eyes after he peeled off his shirt and continued digging in more of a crouching position. The slanted lines of his pelvic bone contrasted with shadows just above the waist of his jeans, and the faint hairs of a treasure trail that subtly percolated from his hardened stomach seemed to ironically point down toward the hole beneath him. The solar shine bounced off his sweat and made his youthful skin and taught muscles glisten with every flexing, pulsating motion.

"Can I get you your water bottle?" she asked as she arched her back, still seated.

He planted his boots on either side of the hole and pompously filled his chest with breath. "Yeah, that would be great."

She heaved herself up and wiggled close. She gazed straight at him and he felt the pull of attraction working its enchanting magic.

She looked at him briefly, then sashayed toward the motorcycle before slowing to a walk and crossing the stream. He leaned his hand against the shovel and found that his eyes automatically drew themselves toward her movements. She had so often complained about the tightness of her jeans, and looking at her now he felt the guilt that he did not share in her complaint, vanish. The bond they had drawn in Nevada seemed not to be loosening, but instead was growing tighter, and it was for him, the easiest folly in the world to fall in love with her, not a weakness to be so wrought upon by her classy, kind, adventurous nature and big heart, by her confident modesty, and musical silhouette, by the liquid depths of her intelligent, perceptive and beseeching eyes or the sweet pout of her lips. He wondered if he would be able to express to her the way she made his stomach into a fluttery of butterflies, and then she promptly looked back at him and smiled, as if she already knew.

He shook himself from his dreamy stupor and kept himself from swooning by clasping his large masculine hands against the hard wood of the shaft and returning his attention back to the hole between his legs.

When she returned with his bottle of water, he thanked her and drank. Hoisting his arm up and tilting his head back, and despite the way she dismissed him, she found herself looking at his neck and once again and longing to place her hands and caress her fingers from the strength of his jawline to the hardened roundness of his shoulders.

With the bottle squirting inadvertently in his eagerness, he transferred it back to her and went on thrusting with wild abandon. Once he had reached a depth of over two feet, the steel of the shovel's blade made an unnatural thud, and a sliver of dark green paint could be seen through the sifted dirt.

Jim went down on all fours and began scraping around the object with care. He continued investigating and found the edges. It was a metal box, a Vietnam era ammo can, and after loosening the earth that surrounded it, he was able to pull it up and out by its handle, surprised by how light it was.

Sam stood next to him and placed her hands on her hips for a moment. She bent over and lowered her body, looking at it, and then glanced at Jim.

He flashed her his crooked smile. "Now it's your turn."

"I'm scared."

"Don't be, I'm here."

The box was about a foot tall and a half a foot wide. She unsnapped the painted metal buckle on the side and opened it. It was mostly empty, and Sam let out a gasp before reaching inside and pulling out a cream colored sheet of paper. She stared at it for a long time and not a word was said. She gave him a look and then studied it again. She put her arm back in the box and found another piece of paper, this time from a yellow legal pad. She unfolded it and read it, and Jim could sense that she was emotional and on the brink of tears.

"What is it?"

She turned toward him, her eyes shining. "I found my wish."

"What?"

She handed him the yellow note. On it was the bubbly writing of a little girl and it said simply, 'a happy home'.

He gave her a sad smile and put his hand on her shoulder. "What's the other thing say?"

She sniffled and took a deep breath. "It's a deed to a house. It's in my name."

They stared at each other in silence. "Where is it?" he asked.

She stood up with both sheets of paper in her hand and drew her eyes westward. "Right there."

Jim gazed in that direction, perplexed. He looked back down at the hole. There was nothing else there.

"Where are they?" she asked.

Jim froze, and searched his pockets and took out the phone. "It's dead."

Sam turned back toward the house to the west. "Let's go."

"There?"

"Yeah."

Jim took hold of the metal box and stepped around the hole and then stopped dead in his tracks. He let go of the ammo can and reached out, holding onto Sam's arm. "Whoa," he said.

He was looking straight ahead at the private drive next to the edge of the forest.

"What?"

"Look," he said with a nod.

Her eyes sharpened and she saw something moving. She looked harder but lost her focus. Then there was movement again and a creature began to take shape. "Is that a…bobcat?" she asked.

Jim's head was fixed. He had heard that lynx and black bears inhabited these lands, but what he was seeing was no bear or lynx. "That's a mountain lion," he said.

It was now clear and the huge cat turned and stared directly at them. It was a beautiful, magnificent creature, covered in a light brown coat of fur with large yellow eyes outlined boldly in black. Jim's instincts were to stay calm and hold his ground so he did nothing but squeeze Sam's arm tighter as the lion stepped forward.

Then a faint rumbling could be heard in the distance and as the seconds passed the rumbling became louder. The cat stopped and turned toward the unnatural noise. Jim's eyes shifted but he did not blink. When he looked back again the lion was gone, but the rumbling was obvious, the sound of motorcycles.

Jim let go of Sam, spun his head around and picked up the ammo can. "Go, go go," he said as he stepped over the hole and pointed himself in the direction of the bike. "Come on, run!"

Sam scampered up the hill while he followed with the box in hand. By the time they reached the motorcycle she was breathless and panting. Jim handed her the box, stuck the keys in the ignition and hopped on the bike in one simultaneous motion. Sam placed her boot on the back floorboards, contorting her leg over the side with the box pressed against her breast. Jim reached down to turn the key but then stopped and listened.

The motorcycles were getting loud enough that Jim knew they had to be on the private drive that was leading directly to their location.

"If we turn back we'll run right into them," he said.

He could hear Sam trying to catch her breath behind him and she said nothing.

Jim turned the keys, held onto the handlebars, paused for another second or two, then rode forward, making a beeline to the house.

They rolled through an open entry gate and Jim instinctively turned right, riding parallel to a high stoney brick wall, approaching a barn on the north side of the house. They blazed through the garage door sized opening and Jim swung the bike around in a 180 degree spin which made Sam nearly lose her grip on the box. He killed the engine, stepped off and Sam followed suit.

Jim stood in the choppy dirt and listened, but heard nothing, the sound of the motorcycles was gone. He turned to Sam. "I'll be right back."

He ran out of the barn, headed to the open outside gateway that was the gap in the brick wall.

When he reached it, he looked out at the private gravel drive that wound its way over the hill and into the forest. Nothing could be seen or heard. He grabbed hold of the cedar plank gate, unhinged its steel fastener and swung it to the center of the opening. He did the same thing with the other side, shoved the metal shaft of the lock down into the designed hole in the ground, pulled a lever that brought the two doors together and latched it shut. He paused and listened again, still nothing. He ran back across the rocky dirt toward the barn, and crouched next to Sam. They stayed quiet, and listened.

A low pitched breathy guttural nicker of a horse broke the silence. Jim looked deeper into the barn and realized that they were inside a row of stables with individual stalls on either side of the opened doored building.

"There has to be somebody living here," he said in a whisper as he twisted his head in Sam's direction. He noticed there was a workbench in the corner, cluttered with tubes of glue, cans of paint and tools.

She swallowed. "Yeah, definitely seems that way."

She rose and walked toward the wide eyed Appaloosa mare in the stall to the left. The horse stepped forward and Sam ran her fingers along the side of its head.

"Who lives here girl?" she cooed under her breath. She looked down the center aisle, there were three other horses in the barn, but many of the stalls were empty.

"You sure this is the right place?" Jim asked after standing up and peeking his head around the edge of the spacious entryway.

"Don't think that matters right now," she said while continuing to pet the horse's muzzle and crest, her eyes darting. "Are they here?"

Jim peered at the brick wall again from where he stood, 30 yards away. Everything was still oddly quiet. "I don't know," he said.

As soon as he finished speaking the clopping sound of hooves could be heard entering the barn from the opposite entrance on the far side. Sam spun herself around and Jim jolted in attention. A man riding a dark brown Morgan was approaching. He stared at them but said nothing, and he rode close and dismounted. He had a split wood bow and a quiver filled with several arrows attached to the side of his saddle. He was older, and dark skinned with long grey hair hanging freely passed his shoulders. He wore a black wide brimmed cowboy hat with a grey ribbon around the crown, and his tan pants were covered by dirty leather chaps. Sam walked over to Jim and stood next to him. She clenched his hand, her fingers trembling. They all looked at each other in excruciating suspense for what seemed like a lifetime.

"Samantha?" the stranger said finally in a deep and stoic voice.

Sam let out a wisp of a gasp and glanced at Jim and then at the man. "Who are you?"

He glared at her and then his wrinkled forehead smoothed. "I was starting to wonder when you were going to show up," he said in a slow, inexpressive tone as he tied the horse to a post to his right, high above its withers. "The place is all ready for you, all you need to do is move in."

"What?" Sam asked with a look of shock and confusion as she watched him fiddle with his ropes.

"What is inside of that box?" he asked as he nodded at the ammo can on the ground next to the motorcycle.

Sam studied him. He was more 50 and seemed to have a permanent frown, but his eyes were clear and focused.

"Who are you?" she asked again.

He finished his quick release halter knot and turned to her. "My name is Warren Pace, I knew your father, knew him very well," he said. "I was sorry to hear that he passed."

Jim squinted. "How did you know he passed?"

Warren tilted his head sideways and up. "He called me just before he went, said he thought he had been poisoned, couple of days later, I received an e-mail from an old friend."

Sam ran her hand against her neck with nervous energy. "Who?"

"Tea Cup," Warren said.

"Tea Cup?" Jim asked.

"Yes, Tea Cup," Warren confirmed.

"Glad to know she survived," Jim said in a murmur of a voice.

Sam was baffled. "You live here?" she asked.

Warren stood still and faced them with his pirarucu Justin's planted firmly in the dirt. "Not exactly," he said. "Let's see what's inside the box."

Sam wrinkled her nose, shifted her eyes at Jim for a second, then bent over and opened the metal container. She took out the deed to the house and showed it to Warren.

He stared at it. "Says here that this place belongs to you."

Jim's eyes were still frozen open. "We ain't got time for this right now," he said as he circled around and focused his attention back to the brick wall outside. He was half expecting for a certain song to begin playing, but there was still nothing.

Warren handed the paper back to Sam. "Were you followed?" he asked.

Jim spun toward him. "There's a lot of people that wanted to see what was inside that box," he said.

"Why?" Warren asked as he scratched the bare skin of his cheek. "It's just a deed to the house, Popeye had a strange sense of humor, but he always had this place in mind for you Samantha."

"Then why," Jim started to say as he lurched forward. "Why bury it?"

Warren looked at him with his brows pulled together. "Because it's always about the journey Jim," he said. "Why are you not wearing a shirt?"

Jim clenched his fists. "It's not a very fun journey when you got a whole army of Iron Raiders chasing you," he said. He grew still and his stare became hazy. "How do you know my name?"

Warren gave him a quizzical grin. "You don't remember me do you?"

The rumbling sound was heard again. Jim whirled around with his eyes on the gate and raised his arm to command silence.

"Did you and Popeye plan for this too?" Jim whispered as the noise of engines became gradually louder and then one by one, shut off.

Warren said nothing. He burbled his lips, adjusted his hat and walked bowlegged and penguin-like out of the barn, his hair swinging as he went. Jim could hear the faint sounds of men talking from beyond the wall. He watched the old man toddle away for a moment, then went into the saddlebags of the motorcycle and took out the Alien. He removed the magazine. There were four, 9 millimeter flat nose bullets left. He inserted it back in with a click, and shoved it into the back pocket of his jeans.

"What do you think you're going to do with that thing?" Sam asked.

"I don't know," Jim said as veins pulsed in his temples. "What do you think the Iron Raiders are gonna do when they find that hole out there with no treasure in it?"

"If they even find it," whispered Sam. "They don't know which tree it is."

"We left a shovel and a hole," Jim said. "They'll find it, and they're not gonna go away until they get what they want."

Snod Farkus was staring at the map and scratching his head, encased in his sleeveless shirt like an overstuffed knackwurst. He looked from the gravel road to the grassy hill that sloped into a rocky cliff and fell into the ocean. He saw the towering redwoods, a grove of eucalyptus trees and the golden orange manzanita.

"Which one is the wishing tree?" he asked. "There are trees everywhere!"

The entire Santa Paula Iron Raiders brigade was there, at least what was left of them. Twelve Harley-Davidson motorcycles, all parked on the private drive on the other side of the gate and the brick wall that surrounded the house. Dice Moya stood next to Snod and followed his eyesight.

"They all look like they could be wishin trees," he said.

Snod opened his chest and pointed himself at the wall. "Tumbleweed!" he yelled. "I know you're around here somewhere!"

Dice focused on the trees below and noticed the white shirt on the ground next to the manzanita. "Prez," he said as he tapped Snod on the shoulder.

Snod stepped forward and squinted. He turned around, took his stahlhelm off and hung it on the handlebars of his chopped out Road King and walked down the hill.

He surveyed the trees and scanned the horizon. The shirt was left balled up at the base of the tree. As he walked closer he noticed the clam shovel and the pile of dirt. He studied the map again. He stomped his boot down and looked up at the drive on the top of the hill. Dice Moya was halfway down the slanting yellowish green grass and the rest of the boys were standing in attention next to their bikes.

"It's gone!" Snod yelled as he began his trudge back.

"Prez," Dice said, motioning his arms.

"What!" Snod yelled as he continued lumbering up the hill.

Dice waited a while for Snod to get closer, and once he had made it all the way back, Dice pointed at the dirt that led to the main gateway of the house.

"Look."

Snod glared at the ground and saw the clear tracks of motorcycle tires going straight under the cedar planks of the gate.

"Tumbleweed!" Snod yelled again.

"Is that Snod Farkus?" A voice said from the other side of the wall. All of the Iron Raiders became silent.

"That's not Tumbleweed," Snod said.

"It's Warren Pace," the voice said.

Snod looked at Dice and then at the gate. "Where's my treasure!"

There was a long pause. "There is no outside treasure that you can take with you," the voice said.

Snod snorted and chortled. "Open the gate!" he shouted as he drew his pistol. "You want to die old man?"

There was another long pause. "There is no death, only change of worlds," the voice said.

Snod turned around and nodded at his battalion of brothers. They all drew their handguns and pointed them at the gate. The men scattered around so that everyone had a clean shot and Snod nodded again and the gate was bombarded with a barrage of bullets. The cedar planks looked like Swiss cheese but the lock held firm and the gate did not open.

"You dead Warren?" Snod asked with a raised eyebrow.

"No, I am still living," Warren said.

"You see the kind of fire power we got," Snod said. "We will get our treasure. You can either give it to us, or we gonna take it. So what's it gonna be?"

There was a moment of silence. "And if I let you in, I will not let you leave." Warren said.

Snod kicked the ground and turned around. "George!" he said. "Bring your bike up here."

George Armstrong nodded and wheeled his supercharged Softail forward and set it down next to Snod. He then went to his saddlebag and took out a heavy iron chain, about four feet in length.

Snod jumped on the bike and fired it up. He directed it toward the wooden gate and revved the engine to its maximum capacity. He looked straight ahead, squeezed the clutch and kicked into gear. He twisted his right hand to full throttle and slid himself back in the seat, then let go with both hands. He stumbled off, and the bike spun forward and slammed into the gate with a splintering smash, blowing the doors wide open. After breaking through, the motorcycle flipped onto its side and walloped into straw bales that were stacked high against the wall at the side of the house.

George charged through the gate, swinging his chain whip like a windmill as he went. Warren Pace was standing, unyielding in his path until at the last second, he ducked down and ran forward. George turned to follow, knowing that he would have him dead to rights between the corner of the brick wall and the bales of straw. George spun and looked, but to his astonishment, Warren Pace was gone.

"Where the," George said in confusion. "I don't get it, he was right here."

An ominous silence seemed to come across the land with a brief and mild gust of wind.

"Somethin' ain't right," Dice Moya said as he turned to Snod. "I got a bad feeling about this Prez."

"Shut up and search the place!" Snod said.

He plodded forward onto the property of the house until he was stopped in his tracks by the echoing sound of a gun going off behind him.

He reeled around and was confronted by the sight of several new visitors with motorcycles parked on the gravel drive abaft from his own crew, boxing the Iron Raiders betwixt the house and their exit.

There was one man slowly walking forward with a handgun pointed skyward. He had long dark hair that was pulled back into a single braid and he wore a black cut with a red patch. Behind him were a dozen or more other men and a few women, all of them wearing similar attire.

225

"Remember me?" the man shouted as he stared at Snod from about forty yards away.

Snod snarled. "You're a dead man Mato."

George Armstrong looked on, from just behind Snod near the gate and straw. He set his chain down and reached for his gun.

Jim Deere crept his way out of the barn, then ran full speed at the wall and jumped, placing his boot halfway up, launching himself skyward. He landed on his knees, high on top of the structure and pivoted to his right. He touched his butt to make sure the Alien was still secure in his back pocket. It was.

He got to his feet and scampered along the top of the wall while trying to stay as low as possible. He could see the confrontation that was happening, with the new group of riders up the drive to his left and the Iron Raiders at the open gate straight in front of him. There was a loose brick laying free on top of the wall directly in his path. He picked it up and started running. As he approached the gate he saw George Armstrong drawing his pistol. Jim clenched the brick in his right hand and decided not to wait for the inevitable shootout to begin below him. He sprinted, reached back and hurled the brick as hard as he could at George.

Just as George was about to pull the trigger and fire a bullet into Mato, he was struck in the temple by the flying slab of stone. His head rocketed to the side and he fell to his right. He dropped his gun and his body convulsed and went limp like a marionette doll without strings. Jim, now at the gate and with no more wall to run on, planted his foot on the edge and vaulted as high and far as he could. He flew overhead of the onlooking Iron Raiders and spun himself around in midair while simultaneously removing his pistol from his pocket and firing a shot at the gas tank of Snod's motorcycle, hoping for some sort of explosion. He missed by a wide margin and landed on his back in the heap of straw.

Several more gunshots followed and Jim rolled to his right between the bales and the south side of the wall. The melodic chirping of birds and soft distant croon of the ocean was now replaced by the repetitive popping and clatter of an all out gun fight. Jim sat up and saw that everyone was shooting blindly and ducking for cover behind their motorcycles in a frantic frenzy. They were all such terrible shots. In a one-percenter outlaw motorcycle club, anyone with an accurate aim is all too quickly accused of being undercover law enforcement, so no one ever really learns to shoot.

Jim caught a glimpse of both Snod and Dice making a run for it on the outside of the wall. After shoving his gun back in his pocket, he crawled to the top of the straw bale and scaled back to the top of the brick structure. He crouched down atop the wall and scurried in the opposite direction of the blaze of gunfire, following Snod and Dice who were fleeing along the outside of the facade below, heading toward the ocean and the far end of the house.

Snod was about 20 feet ahead of Jim, and Dice was just behind Snod. Jim continued to sprint from the wall above, gaining ground on the bulkier more muscle bound men. He launched himself off and soared through the air and descended directly on top of Dice, his boots pummeling into his shoulders.

Dice didn't go down right away and he grabbed onto Jim's ankles and carried him for a few steps until Jim was able to dig his boots into his neck, forcing his body to crumble. Dice tumbled forward and fell on his face while Jim flipped over onto his back. Jim reached for his gun, but before he could, Snod was on top of him.

He was grasping Jim's neck with his left hand and pounding his fist in Jim's face with his right. Jim kicked his knees up and spun around onto his stomach while Snod continued jabbing him in the side of the head. Flinging his legs outward, Jim was able to get himself into a sitting position. Snod wrapped himself around his waist and Jim clenched down on Snod's fingers, bent them backward and rolled onto his side. He put his arm underneath Snod's thigh and pressed his own back against Snod's massive torso, pinning him hard into the rocky dirt.

Composing himself, Dice staggered forward, took out his gun and shoved it into Jim's forehead. Jim closed his eyes, thinking of the worst, thinking of the end, but a whoosh of air whizzed by his ear and the feeling of the hot metal gun barrel on his skin was gone. He opened his eyes. There was an arrow lodged into Dice's arm.

Jim crunched himself down on top of Snod, released him, staggered to his feet, twisted himself around, and saw Sam. She was mounted high on the Morgan, holding a split wood bow in her hand. She reached into the quiver and grabbed another arrow. Snod grabbed a handful of dirt, spun sideways and flung it into her face while bolting to

his feet. He turned and ran like a mad man toward
the front of the house.

Snod stumbled back to where his motorcycle was parked. The shooting had stopped and he found that his entire crew had dropped their guns. He jumped on his motorcycle and started it up. Mato and the rest of Redrum had blocked his exit, so he rode down the hill in the direction of the manzanita tree.

"Get on!" Sam said to Jim, blinking from the dirt and dust in her eyes.

Jim jumped, placing both hands on the back of the horse, lifted himself up and bounced into Sam's back just behind the saddle.

Sam jolted into a trot and then a gallup, following Snod, while Jim clung tight to her waist.

She carefully reached her hand back and gave Jim the bow as she rode.

Jim held on to her with one arm and grabbed an arrow from the quiver with his free hand.

Snod's Road King was not designed for the bumpy terrain beneath him and he struggled along while Sam and Jim breezed closer, gliding with elegance and grace. Snod plowed through the creek, causing him to slow considerably while Sam's horse jumped it in a single bound with ease. Snod now had nowhere to go except off the cliff, into the ocean, and everything seemed to become quiet again, making the singing of the creek and the sputtering of the Harley's engine seem louder.

Jim leaned to the side, away from Sam's back, straddled the horse tightly with his knees, drew back the bow and shot an arrow into Snod. He crashed, right into the hole at the base of the tree. Sam brought the Morgan to a stop and Jim jumped off with the bow still in hand.

Snod rolled in the dirt and whipped around. He drew his gun while on his knees and pointed it at Jim from ten yards away. Jim froze.

"Try anything missy and he gets one in the head," Snod said, glancing at Sam who was a few feet to the left of Jim, still fluttering the dirt and dust out of her eyelashes from atop the horse.

The arrow was sticking out behind Snod in the area around his right shoulder blade. It had punctured through his thick leather vest and shirt but it had not penetrated deep into his flesh. He was breathing heavily, but he gripped his pistol tight with both hands.

Jim stared into the barrel of the gun and gazed at the bulging buggery flaming out of Snod's psychopathic eyes.

"What are you gonna do?" Jim said. "You gonna shoot me, and then what?"

Snod chortled. "Bring me what was buried in this hole and I might let you live."

"There is no treasure," Jim said. "This was just a man leaving his house to his daughter."

Sam circled the horse closer. "And you killed him for it," she said. "All for nothing."

Snod looked up at Sam with his gun still pointed at Jim. "I don't believe you."

Jim lowered the bow. "It's over Snod, you're surrounded, there's no way out of this."

Snod turned to Jim with a sneer. "I can still take you out with me."

There was a long pause. Jim took a step forward.

"It was never about the club was it?" Jim said. "Everything you did you did it for you and you alone and now...look, they turned their back on you."

It was almost true. The Iron Raiders had not literally turned their backs but they had laid down their weapons, and no one was rushing to Snod's defense.

"Everything the club did belongs to me, therefore this be my house, this be my land, and everything on this here property is mine to deal with the way I want to!" Snod said with a stomp of his boot, like a child throwing a tantrum.

As soon as he finished speaking there was a low distinctive and bone-chilling growl that came from somewhere behind him.

Jim looked in the direction of the noise but all he saw was light brown earth and yellow grass. The growl was heard a second time, this time louder than before. Jim looked again, and this time he saw.

The outline of a face perfectly camouflaged by the land was suddenly visible. It was the mountain lion that he and Sam had seen before and it was very near, only a few feet away from the backside of Snod. It was huge up close, bigger than what it should be, nearly 200 pounds, low to the ground, ears erect, and ready to pounce.

The color drained out of Snod's face and he turned his head around in a slow frightened motion. The giant cat took a single step forward and the wind went still and the birds became silent.

The animal's lips drew upward and it showed its savage white teeth. Snod whirled his pistol away from Jim and pointed it at the great cougar.

They looked at each other for a moment, like a standoff of man versus beast. Then the lion leapt and struck in a smooth, powerful blur, clamping it's jaws around Snod's arm. He screamed a terrible screech that echoed across the land for all to hear.

The massive jaws of the creature tore the flesh from his clavicle and humerus like paper-mache, and in what seemed like the blink of an eye, Snod's hulking limb was reduced to bare and naked bone. The cat lifted its blood covered mouth, focusing its yellow eyes on the rest of the Iron Raiders who were standing and watching with slack-jawed dread. All were so shocked and terrified by what they were witnessing that not one of them reached for their guns, they just stood in frozen awe.

The great lion let out a low purr and turned around, stepping on Snod's stomach in the process, and disappearing like a ghost over the cliff facing the ocean. Snod's body fell into the hole next to the wishing tree and his head and neck oscillated in spontaneous spasms.

Jim walked up and stood over him.

Snod peered at the white bone visible in his arm and then looked at Jim. "Hey Halfbreed, did I...did I get the treasure?" he asked in a confused meek wheeze of a voice as the blood gushed from his body.

Jim kneeled down and looked him in the eye. "My name...is Jim."

Snod stared at him and then his gaze became ridged and Jim saw that he was dead.

Jim lifted himself up and looked at Sam before the sound of a sputtering engine drew his attention to the road at the top of the hill. An old pickup truck bumped along and weaved its way between the motorcycles and stopped in front of the blasted open gate near the brick wall. A man and a woman got out.

Jim squinted through the sunlight. He saw that the other group of bikers were indeed Redrum and Redspirit and he recognized both Kima and Mato and he nodded their way.

Dice Moya came running down the hill, bruised and haggard with the arrow still lodged in his arm. He glanced at the body of Snod Farkus and shuttered, putting his hand to his face in horror. He clutched the gun at his side and turned to Jim. Jim stared back and shook his head in defiant fortitude. Dice's face turned sallow and he released his fingers from his holstered pistol.

"I want you to take your boys and go back to where you come from," Jim said as Kima and Mato walked closer. "If I ever see any one of you again, I'll kill you."

Dice let out a wincing breath but said nothing.

"Lick your wounds and go," Jim said, holding his head high and still. "Any man that can't ride and wants to live another day needs to sit on a back seat and be taken with you."

Dice drew his head down and peered at Snod once again. He then turned with a gasp and scampered back up the hill. Kima and Mato were now standing next to Jim in support of his order.

They all watched as the rest of the scraggy Iron Raiders sheepishly mounted their bikes and started their engines. No longer did Jim see them as an intimidating force like he once had. Now they seemed so broken and pathetic. They bumbled out defeated, down the drive and dissolved into the trees as Jim and the rest of Redrum looked on.

As they were leaving, the man and the woman from the truck were walking down the grassy slope. It was the older couple that ran the country store in Honeydew. Jim turned to his right and noticed that Warren Pace had appeared seemingly out of nowhere and was standing next to the wishing tree.

"I called my friends," Warren said as he gestured at the couple. He looked at Snod as he ironically lay dead in the hole of the buried treasure that he sought. "All get what they want, they do not always like it."

Jim was startled by the sight of Warren, as well as by the abrupt oddness of what he said.

"Did you call them too?" Jim asked, glancing at Kima and Mato.

Warren blinked and scratched the side of his face with his index finger. "No."

Kima came closer. "We abandoned our prayer ride when we saw you and Sam leave in such a hurry this morning," she said. "We beat them here, took em by surprise."

"And we saw the motorcycle wrecks you left in your wake back on the 101," Mato said. "Figured there was…trouble."

Jim stared at Warren, still confused. "And where did you go?"

"Told you, I called my friends," Warren said in his usual monotone voice as one of his eyes moved separately from the other.

The old woman from the truck walked a few steps forward and peered down at Snod. "We will just throw the body off the cliff into the sea," she said.

Jim took a breath and studied the lifeless figure in the hole, then turned toward Warren again. "You ever heard of a mountain lion attacking somebody like that round here?"

Warren paused and smacked his lips as if in thought. "No such thing as an ordinary cat," he said.

Kima shrugged. "The west is still wild."

Jim walked over to Snod's tipped over motorcycle as it laid on its side at the edge of the pit of burrowed earth. He almost laughed before he bent down and reached up and under the back fender, pulling out the tracking device. He couldn't help but smile out of all the mixture of emotions he was feeling, holding that little piece of plastic.

"Everything that happened is just because of this stupid thing," he said. "Guess it fooled even Snod."

Kima watched him and her eyes shifted. "The best tracker comes from up here," she said, pointing at her head.

Jim gave her a halfhearted smile and drew his gaze upward to the gleaming blue sky as the Morgan let out an airy whinny.

Warren looked at Sam, still perched atop the saddle. "That's a good horse," he said.

"Yes, he is," she said, shielding the sun with a hand to her forehead while the slight warm breeze blew a wisp of a fairytale curl across her face. "How long have you had him?"

Warren smiled. "He doesn't belong to me."

"Who's the owner?" she asked.

"You are," Warren said. He stepped forward and spread his arms out wide. "All of this belongs to you."

Sam gazed at the property before her. The beautiful trees and rolling yellow fields, the spacious home of Mediterranean style construction, the farmhouse and the old world design of the stables and the vast fenced in greenery of the horse pasture at the edge of the elevated bluff, all overlooking the most spectacular ocean views she had ever seen. It was all so shocking she felt numb.

Jim followed Sam's eyes and then stared at Warren for a long time. "Who are you?"

Warren turned, scrunched his nose and put his thumbs in his pockets. "I'm the caretaker, and a neighbor." He looked to Sam. "I helped your father build and design this place, he knew you loved horses. Of course that doesn't mean you can't sell it, if you want."

Sam sighed deeply and walked the horse around in a slow oval-like motion. "I can't believe it," she said. "I...I had no idea."

"He loved you more than anything," Warren said as he lifted his hat further back on his head. He stuck his finger down the hill behind him, pointing up the coast. "I live in that house, don't know if you can see it over that little ridge there."

Sam saw that there was the corner of a wooden building visible not too far away.

"I didn't know, that he," she started to say before clearing her throat. "I didn't know that he knew me at all."

Jim put his hands on his hips and tilted his head at Warren, still puzzled. "How did you know my name?"

Warren opened his mouth and then closed it, before focusing his eyes downward and remaining silent.

Mato peered up at the rest of Redrum and then tapped Kima on the arm. "We should gather up the group and be on our way," he said. "We're supposed to be up in Klamath soon."

Kima nodded.

Sam jostled her body down from the horse and handed the reins to Warren. She went straight to Kima and they embraced in a hug.

"Thank you so much," Sam said after releasing her arms and taking a step back.

Kima smiled at her while Jim and Mato shook hands.

"Glad you, made it through okay," Mato said.

"Most of us," Jim said, gesturing in Snod's direction.

Mato lifted his brows and exhaled. "Sorry about before, I thought you were one of them," he said, squinting and giving Jim a playful punch on the shoulder. "You know, we could use someone like you in Redrum, guys like us got to stick together. Look to the wind my brother, the nations and the tribes, the greatness of our past, let it not be forgotten. You can ride with us anytime."

"Might take you up on that," Jim said with a short nod. "Guess I'm kind of a nomad now."

Mato grinned before looking at Snod once more. "I always knew I'd see that guy again, maybe just not like this."

"What happened?" Jim asked.

"You see this scar my brother?" Mato said as he ran his finger along his nose. "I had a run in with the Iron Raiders a while back, Snod Farkus did this."

Jim looked to the top of the hill. "What happened up there?"

Mato laughed. "Brother, they can't hit water from a boat, I've never seen anything like it. They're like the neighborhood bully, sometimes all you got to do is fight back, and they collapse like cardboard."

Jim smiled and shook Mato's hand again and then turned and hugged Kima.

"I think I still owe you one," he said.

Kima's eyes twinkled as she brushed back a strand of hair and nonchalantly touched her naked earlobe. Jim noticed from the glare of the sun, the shimmering gold petal shaped earring with a jade center attached to her opposite ear.

"You missing one," he said.

Kima shot her hand away from her face and shifted her weight to one leg. "Yeah, lost it back when I…" She stopped and avoided eye contact. "I lost it down the road somewhere."

Jim looked at her curiously for a moment, then hugged her once again. "Take care," he said.

After Mato and Kima and the rest of Redrum and Redspirit had departed, Warren, the old man and the woman, were left standing by the tree with Jim and Sam. Warren finished tying the horse to a branch of the manzanita and drew his attention back to Jim.

"Popeye tracked me down several years back, after you ran off," he said. "I've known him for a long time, but I didn't know he had you with him. Said he had come across a half native boy from Humboldt County, said he was an orphan, said he had taken him in. I asked what his name was and he says Jim, and I knew it was you."

"Are you my uh…" Jim stammered, looking at Warren, finding it difficult for the words to come out of his mouth.

"I was the chairman of the tribal council for years, so I knew everybody. I'm not a relative but I was there when your aunt moved back to the rez, hoping you might turn up, course by that time you had a life down south, and I knew Popeye was a good man so…" Warren hesitated, gazed at the sky and followed a circling turkey vulture with his eyes. He looked back at Jim, this time with a fire of intensity. "Every young man has a different kind of vision quest."

Jim swallowed, closed his eyes and opened them again. "My great aunt, Lana?" he asked. "Is she...still there?"

Memories were flooding back to him. Images of the woman who had raised him and taken care of him when he was very young, moments long suppressed became vivid in his mind. So much time had passed, he was no more than 6 years old the last time he had seen her.

Warren smiled. "After your father took you, your great aunt moved out, and married this guy who owned a little cafe and general store," he said, slowing his cadence and moving his arms like he was giving sign language. "They run it together now, his name is Tomas."

Jim turned to the old woman and saw that her normally placid stare had become glossy and moist. Suddenly the sun felt like it was burning his eyes and the taste of salt dripped to his tongue and he found that he was crying. The old woman stepped forward and he knew that this was Lana. They hugged, and they hugged for a long time.

"I'm sorry, I should have been there for you after Frankie died," she said.

"It's okay," he said as he placed his hands on her shoulders which seemed much more frail than what he remembered as a child. Time had turned her black hair grey and had made wrinkles around her eyes and mouth, but this was her. This was the caring motherly face that he knew from the earliest of all his memories.

They stepped back from each other, and with their eyes drying, their lips could not stop smiling. Jim fell to his knees, overcome with emotion.

"Well I ah...I suppose," Warren said, not even batting an eye as he turned to Sam. "I suppose I outta show you the house."

Tomas, Lana's husband, adjusted his cowboy hat and came to Jim and put his arm around him. "Now you can move forward, greatness lies before you son. Come on, let's get this done," he said, nodding in the direction of the dead body. He reached out his hand and helped Jim to his feet. "You can grab the legs."

Jim wiped his face and composed himself, then walked into the hole and did as suggested, lifting Snod by the ankles while Tomas took the wrists below the ravaged upper arm. They half dragged, half carried him away from the tree, down to the edge of the cliff that overlooked the ocean.

"You sure about this?" Jim asked.

Tomas took in the view of the horizon. "This is the largest and longest stretch of undeveloped coastline in this country outside of Alaska," he said. "The ocean will clean him and swallow him up forever."

With much strain, they raised Snod off the ground and swung him back and forth and released him over the edge into the Sea Lion Gulch Marine Reserve.

"I've been back and forth from here to my place a lot in the past few months," Warren said as he led Sam in through the main entrance of the house, with Lana following. "Popeye bought this land years ago, but didn't have the house built until... 20..yeah 2019."

Sam looked up at the natural wood timber framed ceilings, then down at the bamboo flooring that changed to caramel colored Saltillo tiles as she entered the Spanish style kitchen after passing beneath a cream colored stucco archway. The rooms were spacious, and there was an exposed brick fireplace, a solid cherry dining table and two traditionally designed sofas upholstered in velvet.

"It's furnished," she said as her eyebrows curved upward. The place was rustic and beautiful, and cute beyond her expectations.

"Yeah, some old antique type stuff," Warren said as he weaved into the living room. "Little sparse right now, but open for you to, you know... do what you want."

"I know of a good little store not too far away, if you need anything," Lana said with a warm smile.

Sam ran her fingers through her hair and then tugged on her tank top. "I could use some new clothes," she said, turning around, just beyond the kitchen counter and looking at Lana.

"We sell some clothes too ya know," Lana said as all three of them stood near the fireplace.

"It's like, ready to be rented out," Sam said observing the quaint design of the interior and the amenities that were scattered about in the kitchen and living room. The place made her apartment in Sedona look like a prison cell. "This is incredible."

Warren shot her a coy smile. "Wait till you see the view."

He walked to the sliding glass door at the back wall that was almost nothing but windows and exited onto the ironwood decking that wrapped around the ocean side of the house. Sam and Lana followed.

The sweeping panorama of the shining blue Pacific seascape was overwhelming. The house and deck was roosted several hundred feet above the water level, making it possible for the breathtaking sights to stretch far and wide in all directions. Oregon was somewhere off to the right, Point Reyes and the Golden Gate beyond the King Range to the left, and Japan perhaps straight ahead, far beyond the defined line of the horizon beneath the sun.

"It's, just amazing," Sam said, genuinely astounded. "But I don't know if I can afford to maintain it or…"

"Your father said you might like to run a trail riding business of some kind," Warren said, leaning on the waist-high railing at the edge of the deck. "I'd be happy to help with that, if that's what you want to do."

Sam didn't know what to say. This was the dream house that well surpassed her wildest fantasies of imagination. It was more than she could comprehend or digest all at once.

She sighed, standing next to Warren. "Horses are so expensive to care for."

He let go of the wooden barrier as a soft breeze flowed through the grey hair beneath his hat. "Well, I should probably show you another thing."

"What?"

He looked at her for a second, patted his hands on the railing a few times and meandered back inside. All three of them were in the kitchen when Jim and Tomas entered the house through the front door.

Warren stopped and chuckled at the sight of them. "I'll let you guys wash your hands."

Sam watched as Jim rubbed his palms together and she made a squeamish face of realization as to what he and Tomas had just done. "Oh my gosh," she said under her breath, looking at Jim.

"I'm going to show Sam something real quick in private, we'll be back out in a minute," Warren said.

"I'll make some coffee," Lana said. "If you don't mind Sam."

Sam shook her curious smirk away from Jim and turned toward Lana with a sweet smile. "No, please, coffee sounds great."

Warren took her down a slant ceiling skylighted hallway and through an arched doorway that led to a large Persian carpeted room with a fully made-up king-sized bed. He closed the door behind them, went to the far wall, unlocked and opened a light brown oak wardrobe and took out a big metal box, the same style, but larger than the one that she and Jim had dug up next to the wishing tree.

He placed it on the mattress and looked Sam in the eye. "I know Popeye had a thing for buried treasure and stuff but didn't seem right to keep cash in the ground like that."

Her eyes widened. "What do you mean?"

He opened the box and she stepped forward and looked inside. It was filled to the brim with yellow sealed stacks of flat, crisp, one hundred dollar bills in bundles. She lifted her head up slowly.

She gasped. "Is this from...is this from the um...Axis San Diego thing?"

His expression changed. "What do you know about that?"

"Paula...or Tea Cup told me the story, about how three men on motorcycles, robbed a bank or something...1992?"

He took off his hat, threw it on the bed and put his hand to his chin.

"That was a long time ago, this money here is clean as a whistle," he said as he paced around in a tight circle. "That bank was an evil corporation anyway."

"So it's true?"

He stopped. "Yeah, I cannot lie, it is true."

"Three men?"

He cleared his throat. "Yes."

"Who were they?"

He sighed and they sat down on the mattress together. He squeezed his eyes shut. "Well, uh...one of them used the money to help his own people, bought some land and donated much of it to his reservation," he said. He opened his eyes. "Another one used it to get married and open up a little country store, which he still runs with his wife to this day."

Sam swallowed and stared at the side of his face. "And the third?"

He looked at her, reached back and slid the ammo can between them. "The third well he…he used a good amount to buy a huge piece of property and build a house that he wanted to leave for his daughter, the rest of his share is what's in this box, and now it belongs to you."

She touched the money with the tips of her fingers, trembling. "How much is this?"

"2 million, give or take a thousand," he said. "It's all yours to use how you want."

She stood up, stepped off the rug and onto the soft bamboo flooring and then back to the rug, bitting her cuticles. "I don't uh…this house is more of a treasure than I could have ever hoped for."

He looked down at his feet and then up again. "Popeye got sucked into something very bad," he said with emotion weighing heavy in his voice. "But what you and Jim did today, changed that for the better. Now you can use what your father left behind, to turn it around and make things good, change his legacy and make your own."

She stood very still and sat back down on the bed. "This house and this box, it's all that's left of him," she said.

He became very quiet. "Aren't you forgetting something?"

"What?"

He turned his head toward her, and a single tear rolled down his cheek. "You."

Her lips quivered as she looked at the carpet and they were still trembling when she looked at him. She sniffled, wiped her eyes, then she and Warren stood up and hugged. She let out another whimper and, being so overwhelmed with emotion, started laughing. She took a few steps back and spun around in astonishment.

"So the stories about his treasure were true the whole time," she said walking over to the box.

He smiled.

*"I'm a rolling stone just rolling on
catch me now 'cause tomorrow I'll be gone."*

Hours later, after Tomas, Lana, and Warren had all gone home, Jim and Sam were left to themselves, their bellies still full from the Carnitas Huevos Rancheros and Sopaipillas that Tomas and Lana had made in a whim of celebration. With herbal tea, they sat side by side on a bench on the back deck, watching the sun slowly dip its way into the ocean.

"I'm happy for you," Sam said with both hands on her warm ceramic mug. A strong feeling of loneliness overpowered her. "Happy you found…family."

Jim gazed at her. Her hair was still wet from her shower. Wearing the same jeans she bought back in Kanab, she had changed out of Kima's top into Jim's only other white t-shirt, freshly washed and straight out of the dryer. "The last few days have been," he said in a mumble after a sip of tea. "I don't know what to call it."

"What?" she asked, shifting closer.

He cleared his throat. "I said I don't really know what to make of the past couple days, it feels surreal…like a…like a dream."

"Yeah, I keep thinking I'm gonna wake up soon," she said in a somber coo. "I still feel kind of numb...just like, in shock or something."

He became quiet for a while, holding tight to his cup. The feelings of joy and happiness were foreign and uncomfortable to him as were the feelings of loving someone and the possibility of being loved back. They had reached their destination and he was so happy that he was miserable, considering happiness as a fleeting emotion, as he was so accustomed to never staying put, and having nothing to lose, leaving those he loved only with footprints, and taking with him only memories. An old poem came into his mind and a wave of melancholy swept over him. He remembered the words and went over them in his head.

> *I was in your presence for*
> *an hour or so*
> *Or was it a day?*
> *I truly don't know*
> *Where the sun never set,*
> *where the trees hung low*
> *By that soft and shining sea*
> ...something something
> *In the summertime, when*
> *you were with me...*

He thought about how, as in everything romantic, it was written in the past tense; when you were with me. He turned to her. "What are you going to do, you gonna stay here?"

She looked out at the hazy sun as it darkened a deeper orange with its lower half hidden beneath the Pacific's horizon line. The

251

evening was still warm, and the wandering wisps of breeze did not stir the slumber of the air. "All I want right now is peace and quiet. This might be the most peaceful place on earth."

"It'll be dark soon," he said, deeply focused on the glossy hot water of his tea. "I should probably head out."

She spun her head toward him with the whites of her eyes prominent. "What?"

He stroked his jaw and lowered his brows. "This is your house, not mine."

"Oh no you don't," she said as she arched her back and swiveled her knees so they were almost touching his. "I am not about to stay in this place all by myself after what just happened. You don't have any place to go anyway."

"Yeah but," he started to say as his gaze went from the ocean and then directly into her eyes. "We, we barely know each other."

She placed her hand on his kneecap with a gentle tenderness and studied his face for a long time. His bruises and scars were palpable, but they did not detract from the handsomeness she saw in him. "I know you well enough for now," she said as a smirk formed on her lips. "I know that you'll do anything to protect me, even when it puts your life in danger. I know that you are kind, and thoughtful. I know that you want something more out of life than…than a lot of other people do."

She spoke in a slow soft tone that seemed to sooth him and she lifted his chin up with her fingers and went on. "I know that you bite your cheek and get all hunched over when you're nervous."

He blushed and ran his hand through the hair above his ear. "You only know the good things," he said. His shoulders tensed. "This is all yours, I don't want to burden you...you should start new, you said yourself you liked the idea of starting fresh."

She buried her gaze into his brown eyes, one of which was surrounded by a purple bruising that was turning black. "Jim, I wouldn't be here if it wasn't for you. If it wasn't for you, those guys would've eventually tracked me down, and I'd probably be dead."

"I don't know, I keep thinking I just led them to you," he said as he fidgeted with the short sleeves of his shirt. "Makes me sick thinkin about it."

"Stop it," she said, placing her hand on his wrist. "It's not like I was exactly happy...really, I mean before. I could never have imagined all this or everything that was going to happen, but, um... I needed a change and...I have never felt more alive than I did when I was riding with you, I have no idea what my dad was thinking but..."

He put his tea down on the wooden decking. "I think he was oblivious to what was going on in his own crew." He paused. "Men only covet things that are difficult to attain...he had gotten too far removed from those guys."

"Unless he just wanted you to find me." Her eyes were glowing. "Wanted me to come here with you, I mean he knew you were from here, he knew I loved it here, it's not a coincidence."

He shook his head. "There's no way he could have known all of what, all of what..."

"Stop, it's okay," she said, getting still after clasping the inside of his forearm again. "Warren gave me a truck to use, I have more money than I could ever spend, the house is furnished, the bed has um, bedding, I don't need you to stay here…I want you to stay here, I want you to stay with me."

He nodded slow, peering at the fiery sky, now turning purply pink. He turned to her, his eyes burning with hopeful longing as he marveled at her very presence. Both inside and out, her loveliness was not at all subtle, it was overt and indisputable. His voice lowered and softened into a whisper of sentimentality. "It's gorgeous here."

Her eyes expanded with the sharp focus, intensity and conviction in the way he was looking at her. "Yeah, I just want to enjoy it tonight and forget everything," she said, putting her cup down to her left and delicately sliding her hips to her right, pressing her thigh softly into his. She let out a sweet and breathy sigh. "Maybe we'll laugh about it all someday, but for now I um, just want to…"

She trailed off and her shoulder touched his arm as lightly as a butterfly touches indigo. She was drawn by some force more powerful than gravity, strong as destiny. The feeling of her touch sent a tremor through his body and shivers down his spine. His arm began to steal around her and behind her. A fever of expectancy seemed to raise her body temperature, her lips moist and hot and her pulse leaping. She lowered her head onto his chest and he cradled the soft skin of her cheek with a hand so gentle and protective that she felt she could have collapsed into his arms and stayed there with never another desire or worry for the rest of her life.

"I don't think I have ever felt like this before," she said after a long period of silence.

"Me too."

Jim slept late into the following morning, waking from the radiant brightness of light that came streaming through the huge bedroom windows, despite their west facing layout. Sam stirred dreamily beneath the comforter, her freely tumbling brown hair falling in romantic waves over plush white pillows. She looked too peaceful for him to rouse her, so he let her rest, threw on his jeans and boots and quietly slunk into the kitchen.

He opened the fridge and investigated its contents. There was a tray of farm fresh eggs from Warren's chickens, a half-gallon glass bottle of whole milk, a block of Irish butter and a jar of Aunt Lana's homemade blueberry jam. On the Spanish tiled countertop there was a glass container of white flour and another one of sugar. In the cupboards he found coarse sea salt, and hanging beneath was a wide and shallow frying pan. He could not find baking powder but he had everything he needed to make pancakes, so that's what he did.

Cooking was a revelation for him and he also had an inability to relax and felt a certain need or obligation to earn his keep, or perhaps, and more likely, he just wanted to do something nice for Sam. The pancakes turned out horribly, not at all like he planned. They were way too thin, and

Jim found that when he held one up to the light he could see right through it. He panicked and scrambled to to arrange his failed breakfast into a somewhat presentable form.

When she finally rose from bed and wandered into the kitchen, awakened by the smell of Chinese coffee and melted butter, she was stunned to be greeted with a steaming hot plate of French style crepes folded into quarters and overlapping each other like rose petals dripping in a sauce of wild blueberries.

"Oh my goodness," she said, rubbing her eyes and yawning with a knitted blanket draped over her shoulders. "You made crepes?"

He nervously ginned and led her to the circular wooden table, complete with a view of the ocean, where their breakfasts were waiting. "This house really did come ready to go didn't it," he said.

"I guess so." She sat down and breathed in the divine smells. "You never told me you could cook."

He pulled a chair up beside her as she promptly slid her fork between her lips. "Oh, I didn't mention that when we went on our first date?"

"No, you didn't," she said with a giggle. "You were too busy swinging a helmet into somebody's face, and then taking me all the way to Utah on the back of a motorcycle...after my car exploded."

"You consider that our first date?" he asked after he finished chewing.

She took another bite and let her blanket slip away. "Doesn't matter, these are delicious, and I've decided that I want to keep you around."

Jim blushed and slowly put food into his mouth. Sam pulled out a cookbook from the shelf against the wall to her right, 'How To Be A Domestic Goddess'.

"This place really does have everything," she said, gazing at the hardcover and then smearing her crepes around in the sweet jam. "Totally could rent this out once in a while, if we ever want to travel."

"We?"

"You're a good person to travel with."

"So are you," he said, peering at the book. "But ain't you ready to have a home...be a um domestic goddess?"

She smiled. "Maybe...but that doesn't mean that we have to be done traveling. There's still so many places I want to go. I've never even been to Oregon."

"I always wanted to go to Puyallup, Washington. They say it's the largest city in the world that both begins and ends with the letter 'P'."

"Sounds amazing."

Jim nodded and took a sip of coffee. "Warren was sayin there's a Salmon Festival up at the rez next month, 5k fun run and a fair and stuff, ain't too far from the state line. Might be a good excuse to go north."

She licked her mouth. "I'd definitely be into that."

He watched as she went back to devouring her breakfast with such alluring enjoyment and bliss. "Never...thought of myself ever being, domesticated," he said.

"Mm...well, you're really good at making breakfast. We shall have to see if there's a book about, How To Be A Domestic God." She smacked her lips and looked at her plate, already half empty and covered in a buttery purple glaze of jam. "Ooh, I always hate it when I eat too fast and then everything is almost gone when the other person is like just four bites in."

"Sorry, I'm too slow."

"No, I'm the one who needs to ease up and just like, savor each bite," she said. She seductively batted her long eyelashes and sighed with dreamy and voluptuous rapture. "But it's just not the same when I control myself. I think I just prefer being... flooded with pleasure."

Jim went flush as his mind vanished into her character and into her heart, getting lost in her chocolate eyes and the living breathing work of art that was her face and spirit within. She was so beautiful, and Jim loved beauty passionately, but more than beauty, he loved Sam.

They ate until they were full and completely satisfied and it was very good. And once done and after cleaning up and getting ready for the day at a leisurely pace, they headed down to Honeydew in the rusty 1973 Ford F-250 Warren left them.

They had lunch and visited with Tomas and Lana, drank more coffee and Sam picked out some new clothes. The options were limited but she settled on a few brightly colored tourist shirts, a knit long sleeve sweater, as well as a yellow sundress, a pair of leggings, pajama bottoms, socks and underwear while Jim got a pack of t-shirts and stocked up on groceries. They figured they could head over to Eureka or Santa Rosa on a later day to do more substantial shopping, but for the time being, rest and relaxation were priorities.

When they arrived back at the house, Warren was there, finishing up feeding the horses and walking toward them from the barn as they stepped out of the truck.

"Took Spots for a little ride just now, there's a trail that traverses down the bluff where there's a secluded little beach, just right down there straight ahead," he said as he pointed in the direction of the ocean. "You should take her and Rod, it's a gorgeous ride."

Warren had explained earlier that the Appaloosa was named Spots and the Morgan was named Rod, and although the horses could graze freely on the lush grass of the vast enclosed pasture, he often supplemented their diet with concentrates and occasional salt from the confines of the stables.

"Really?" Sam asked with the shopping bag of clothes in hand, while Jim banged down the tailgate and grabbed the groceries.

"Sure, they're your horses," Warren said. "If you take some wood you can have a campfire on the beach, few things in life better than that."

She smirked at Jim before looking back at Warren. "We just might do that."

"I'm going to head back."

He went over to his more modern black F-150 and yelled, "Call me anytime though."

After shouting their thanks, Sam and Jim went inside the house and flung their things on the kitchen counter. Sam went to the living room and collapsed on the couch and Jim sat down next to her.

"Mmmm, so sleepy," she cooed as she leaned back and curled her calves beneath her thighs.

"Might just set up a chopping block with them logs out front, like he was sayin, fire on the beach sounds nice if you're not too tired."

She covered her mouth with the back of her hand and yawned. "Yeah, that does sound nice. We should have bought some marshmallows."

"I'd be happy to go back to the store."

"You're sweet," she said as she brushed back her hair with her fingers. "I like you Jim Deere."

"I like you too, Sam Diego."

She slid deeper into the sofa. "I enjoyed riding with you, I almost miss it already."

"Yeah, get a taste of adventure, and it will just call you for the rest of your life."

She sat up a little. "Rest of my life, adventuring and exploring with you?"

"Well, I don't um…"

"I like the sound of that."

She smiled, although as he looked into her pure limpid eyes again, he was suddenly self-conscious of his bruises, as if her flawless features brought to light an awareness of his own unworthiness.

She reached forward and gently caressed the swollen purple flesh above his cheek bone. "You need to let me put some ice on that."

"Later," he said, blinking and placing his hand on her knee. "You rest, I'l be out front, choppin stuff."

She intentionally fluttered her lashes and turned away slightly while maintaining eye contact. "Can't wait to teach you to ride a horse."

"Lookin forward to it," he said after rising to his feet. The pull of his magnetism to her seemed more than he could bare, and he felt he needed to focus all his masculine energy on something other than these unfamiliar sensations of transparent love that were throbbing in his heart and pulsing in his veins. As he walked away, out to the barn, his face broke into a smile so big it hurt.

"Keep your toes pointed up," Sam said as she watched Jim struggling with his horse.

He sat atop the Morgan while she was on the Appaloosa, just leaving the stables.

"How do I steer?" he asked as he and his horse began wandering aimlessly away.

"Just give the reins a tug in the direction you want to go." She trotted toward him on the back side of the barn near the fenced in pasture. She rode with such control and beauty and he watched closely with adoring admiration. "You're okay, these guys are well trained, pretty lazy actually and low key."

The Morgan jolted forward. "Whoa," he said. She smiled, observing that he looked more anxious now than he ever did in the past four days. "Not used to being this high up," he added as he adjusted the straps of his backpack filled with picnic food, which was rubbing up against a small bundle of firewood tied to the saddle.

"You got the right boots for it," she said, observing his attire of Noconas, jeans, and the brown leather jacket. "Just need to get you a cowboy hat." She instantly felt silly after she said that. "Or I don't know…"

"Just because I'm an Indian don't mean I can't wear a cowboy hat." His nerves began to calm as he twirled in a circle.

"But you're not Indian, you're Native American."

"Yurok." He jostled into a brisk walk, heading for the far side of the field.

She caught up with him quickly. "Don't grip with your legs so much," she said before breezing by him and out the open gate onto the trail. Wearing her new black yoga pants, she slid herself backward on her saddle and patted her thigh. "Communicate more with your butt."

He came up fast right behind her as the path narrowed and started its descent toward the ocean. "How do I stop?" he asked in a worried voice.

She lifted her reins and rolled her eyes. "Just pull back."

She turned and broke into almost a canter as she traversed downward. He followed her with caution, although he was fast becoming more comfortable and confident with every clip clop of the horse's hooves. He was amazed by how smooth the ride was, considering the jagged unevenness of the ground, and he felt as though he could go anywhere.

The patches of Douglas-fir and Tanoaks faded into the yellow green of coastal prairies as they descended closer to the shoreline. The path drew steep and veered south, running parallel to the bottom of a cliff a few hundred feet below the house. They continued up and over a small rocky hill covered in Knobcone Pines, and then the waves of the ocean came into view, breaking and crashing on a secluded cove that beveled into a white beach with the sound of the surf competing for dominance with the mewing of seagulls.

To Jim's amazement, Sam lifted her butt up above the saddle and galloped into a four beat gait, right onto the sheen of the wet arenaceous seaboard, leaving him far behind. He kicked his heels into Rod's sides and went after her. His speed increased as he zigzagged the path and leveled onto the beach, the bundle of wood bouncing behind him. Salty sea air filled his lungs and nostrils. He sat tall and centered his weight on the stirrups and squeezed his boot heels inward. Rod took off and Jim felt as though he were flying, the dull rhythmic thud of the hooves tossing back sand and water as he hugged the shallows of the thin and even tide waters.

Sam stopped and spun the Appaloosa around once she reached the towering jagged rocks that put an end to the beach, and Jim tugged on his reins and leaned back as Rod slowed to a trot then a walk.

"Wow," she said. "Not bad for a first timer."

"Had a good teacher," he said with a huge grin before making a wide slow turn. He took a deep refreshing breath and gazed at the waves smashing beneath the sunset, then looked back at her. "This is amazing, I don't think I could ever get tired of this."

She smiled and drew her eyes inland. "See that Candelabra tree?"

"Oh wow."

"Meet you there!"

She gently slapped Spots' crest and bolted in the direction opposite the ocean where the beach ended and grass began, her hair blowing soft and free. The Candelabra redwood she pointed out was magnificent, with branches twisting and turning upward from a massive gnarled trunk, making it a perfect hitching post.

After securing Spots and Rod and unloading the bundle of wood, Jim made a fire pit on the beach, moving and lifting rocks into a circle. He configured the split logs and kindling into the shape of a tepee and stuffed newspaper scraps in the center and lit it to flames with the stick lighter from the backpack Warren had lent them.

By the time the fire had collapsed into a gentle glow of coals, the sun was gone and the evening dimmed velvety hues of gold and red. They roasted bratwursts on a couple of stiff twigs, and ate under the stars as the ocean waves became just an invisible tranquil sound in the distance while the crackling pine and mesquite sweetened the cooling air.

"What did you ever do with that guy's phone?" Sam asked as she sat on a long thick piece of driftwood close to the warm fire and hip to hip with Jim.

"It's charging up in the house, don't even know why...should probably just throw it away," Jim said with his mouth still full of food.

She sighed deeply, looking down, holding the end of her bun and shifting the sand around with her boots. "I still can't believe all that, so crazy."

He nodded.

"Glad we did this though," she said before finishing the last of her perfectly charred bratwurst and turning toward him. "Mm...should have brought some champagne to celebrate."

265

"Yeah, that would've been um good." His eyes slumped toward the ground. "I'm sorry I gotta tell ya, I um, don't do too well with alcohol."

"You a lightweight like me?"

"No no, it ain't that," he said as shame filtered burdensome in his voice. "It's more just that it gets me into trouble, so better I just tell you now."

"What kind of trouble?"

"Like I'm allergic and break out in handcuffs."

She sensed the sorrow and regret in his voice. "Oh."

"Kinda embarrassing, it ain't easy for me to admit that."

She placed her hand on his neck. "It's okay, everybody has something that they struggle with. I don't need champagne, I really don't care, just being with you is enough."

He nodded and smiled with relief and appreciation. "Thanks."

She stared at him for a long time. "Does it feel weird, being free, you know like…no more motorcycle club and everything?"

"Well, there's always Redrum."

"Yeah, I guess it is nice to have somebody looking out for you."

He gazed up at the stars, looking for constellations that might impress her while she nestled her head against his shoulder.

"What next?" he asked. "You gonna start a trail riding business?

"Maybe."

"It's your dream right?"

"Yeah," she said, sitting up and adjusting her posture. She looked at him. His eyes and week's worth of facial stubble were highlighted by the smoldering fire against the night sky and he bent his arm, feeling his shoulder with his hand, his bicep crawling out from under his shirt sleeve into a knot of muscle, heavy and hard. "But I can't do it alone."

He drew his head close to her's, their noses only inches apart. "Do you um, know of anyone that could help?"

"I can think of someone," she said in a whisper.

"Who?"

"I haven't um, I haven't known him for very long and he has very little experience with horses…"

"So why him?" He put his arm around her, caressing her soft shoulder with his hand.

"Oh…um, well, he's very kind and, he's a very fast learner, he knows a little construction, he knows how to weld, just in case I like need some help around the house and with the stables," she said, as her voice turned whimsy. "Also he's not a gang member, and I'm pretty sure he's all done screwing around and hanging out with low-lives by now."

"Why do you think he's done?"

She looked straight into his eyes. "Because he has something a lot better than that in his future. Of course though…I think he has it in his mind that he wants to be a nomadic free spirit with nothing to lose."

There was a moment of serene tenderness between them. "I guess he'll have to change his plans," he said with a rasp of emotion as he pressed her body against his. A great temptation assailed him. He had caught glimpses of adoration in her eyes and he wanted more than anything to tell her he loved her, and the words trembled on his lips. "But do you really think it's a good idea to work with someone who's in love with you?"

She was unfazed and didn't miss a beat. "I don't care, I just want to spend time with him."

"And I just want to spend every minute with you," he said, nudging his legs slightly closer and breaking their playful third person banter. He cleared his throat. "Workin with horses is a good idea though."

"Why is that?"

"If nothin else…it's a stable job."

She stared at him blank faced. A hint of a smirk formed on her lips but she refused to laugh. "It's okay, I'm sure you're funny too."

He smiled and she clung to him, unable to release herself, and he sat, half supporting her in his arms as her body made its happy, nestling movement.

"I don't think the treasure my father wanted to give me was the money," she said after a pause.

"Yeah it was the house."

"No, I don't think it was that either."

He sighed. Several times he was about to speak and each time he hesitated, until finally he asked, "What was it?"

She lowered her head deep into his chest and softly cooed, "This."

He held onto her tight and snug while shooting stars flew back and forth like a frenzy of hockey pucks. Not a word was spoken, and not a word was spoken for a long time.

"We should go," she said finally. "It's getting cold."

"Yeah." He stood, and then helped her to her feet. He grabbed his jacket and let her slip her arms through. "Is there any, trick…to riding in the dark?"

"Trust the horse, I think they know these trails pretty well."

Jim threw some sand on the fire and they packed up and climbed into their saddles. Sam led and he followed, and they rode carefully up the hill back to the house. Jim fidgeted with his posture. He had forgotten that the tracking device was still in his pocket and it was digging into his thigh quite uncomfortably. His mind wandered. He somewhat regretted what he said before about the champagne and thought about how maybe it would be nice to have a drink or two with Sam on the back deck. After all, he had done more than he imagined he could, and he was a different person than he was just a few days ago.

He thought of his own father's struggle with alcohol, as well as Popeye's involvement with the program. Popeye used to say that even during abstinence, the alcoholic demons, (as he called them) are still waiting outside your door, doing pushups and getting stronger. Jim wondered if that applied to him. The disease of the Iron Raiders was gone, he was safe now and cured of their infectious germs.

They entered in the far side of the stables, but were stopped cold by the sight of a figure standing next to a motorcycle on the far end of the barn.

"Who's that?" Jim shouted.

"It's Kima."

"Kima, what are you doing here?" Sam asked.

"I just want to talk."

Jim and Sam looked at each other curiously.

"Okay, hold on," Sam said. She dismounted and Jim did the same. She gave him her reins. "I'll go see what she wants if you can take care of the horses."

Jim nodded. "Yeah, okay."

He watched Sam walk away with Kima, disappearing into the house. He couldn't put his finger on why, but something about the situation didn't feel right. His mind was going to surprising places as he led Spots and Rod to their stalls. He kept peering at Kima's motorcycle and the blue bungee cords wrapped around the sissy bars. He struggled with Spots, and while trying to keep her calm he felt the tracking device rubbing against his thigh again. He shoved his hand in his pocket and removed it, turned around and tossed it on the workbench in the corner of the barn.

*"Should we lose each other
in the shadow of the evening trees
I'll wait for you, should I fall behind
wait for me."*

"Yep," Kima said as they entered the bedroom.

Sam sat on the mattress. "So what brings you here so late?"

Kima stared at her blankly. "I would like to have my shirt back."

"Really?" Sam asked, confused. "You came all the way here for that?"

Kima placed her right hand beneath the front of her vest, pulled out a tiny Beretta Tomcat pistol and spastically pressed it into Sam's head. "And the rest of your daddy's money...scream and I'll shoot."

Sam jolted erect in her seat, her hands rushing to her sides and clutching the comforter, flabbergasted and stunned. Her breathing accelerated, and bewildered, she gently turned her head toward Kima. "You are not going to kill me."

Kima looked her in the eye, the kindness in her face was gone and replaced by venomous vile that Sam had never seen in her before.

"Are you willing to bet your life on that?" Kima asked.

Sam gasped and drew her hands slowly upward, then rose.

"Don't worry, it's only money," Kima said as Sam made her way to the oak wardrobe.

Kima kept her gun within inches of Sam's back and watched her fiddle with the combination of the lock. The wardrobe opened and Sam became very still.

"What are you going to do with it?" she asked, staring at the ammo can with her back to Kima. She felt the Beretta as it pressed hard into her spine.

"You don't need to worry about that."

Sam spun around holding the box of cash and shoved it into Kima's arms, staring at her with blazing eyes. "You can have it all, take it and leave."

Kima nearly dropped her gun. She looked at Sam briefly, but she could not maintain eye contact.

"I've been looking for this for a long time," Kima said finally.

There was another long pause. "What about Mato and Redspirit?" Sam asked.

"Sam!" Jim's voice rang out from the foyer.

Kima set the ammo can down on the floor and pointed the gun at Sam, while keeping a close eye on the bedroom door. Seconds later Jim Deere walked in.

He froze and his heart dropped to his stomach. "What's going on?"

"Get over there, move!" Kima said, shifting the gun back and forth between them.

Jim stood next to Sam. He was speechless.

"I'm glad you're here...halfbreed," Kima said. "Billy is alive by the way, told me you tried to kill em."

Jim cleared his throat, dumbfounded. "Redspirit plan this, Mato? Who are you?" he asked in a stream of hesitant dither.

"You really have no idea do you," Kima said as a demonic smile composed its way out of her cracked lips and vacant eyes. "Mato, Redrum, Redspirit they're all schmucks. Mato is so into spreading positivity on two wheels that he'll just let anyone infiltrate his crew."

"You a cop?" Jim asked.

Kima broke into a harsh laugh. Still pointing the gun, she lifted her shirt sleeve with her free hand, revealing a tattoo of a smiling skull and crossbones on the leathery tan skin of her upper arm. "Popeye never told you much about the North Phoenix chapter did he? We do things a little different, we play a very long and patient game."

"What?" Sam said under her breath.

Kima's eyes flamed hideous impropriety. "Well, we certainly weren't gonna let Snod Farkus and those Santa Paula idiots get Popeye's treasure, but we were happy to let you and them do our dirty work, led us straight to it, just like we planned."

Jim stepped between Sam and Kima's pistol. "Let Sam go."

"What you think I'm going to kill you two? Oh no, no, I want you and Sam to go on living, knowing full well that Bronson Barrera and the North Phoenix Iron Raiders got the best of you." She reached down and picked up the ammo can. Holding it with one hand and pointing the gun with the other, she stepped backwards. "So...

resolve with peace, and travel in peace Jim and Sam, and just remember I warned you, the West is still wild."

She turned, exited through the sliding glass doors of the bedroom, onto the outdoor decking and disappeared out of sight.

Jim and Sam stared at each other for a second and quickly embraced in a hug of alleviation and disbelief.

Still racked with fear, but overcome by curiosity, they went out to the front of the house moments later. Kima's motorcycle was no longer there. They stopped and listened but could hear nothing.

"She's gone," Sam said, both dejected and relieved, looking up at the stars. She let out a short laugh of hysteria and perturbation. "I can't believe it, I thought she was my friend." She grabbed Jim's arms. "She was playing us the whole time."

He took a deep breath, reached into his pocket and took out a gold petal shaped piece of jewelry.

"What's that?" She asked.

"Her other earring, found it on the ground way back in Arizona, even before I found you. Had it in my saddlebag." He gestured toward his Indian which was parked just a few feet away. "Took it out when you and Kima were inside, just startin to put it together."

"So she was…following you all the way from L.A.?"

"Hang on." He ran away from her, into the house. When he came back out he was holding Boone's cell phone. He shrugged, wide-eyed. "Well, we better go after her then."

She looked at him, perplexed, and made a movement of dissent. "Yeah right, where? To Phoenix? She's gone, she'll vanish like she did in Nevada, we're never gonna see her or that money again."

"Sure we will." He showed her the screen.

She saw the red dot moving slowly across a map of the surrounding area. "The tracker?" she asked, her eyes expanding large. "Is that…"

"It's on her bike."

She squished her lips together in pensive bemusement. "How did you…"

"Gut instinct, I wasn't expecting anything like this to happen, but, had a hunch…somethin told me somethin wasn't right with her, I mean I don't even know."

Sam had the same fire burning through her eyes that Jim had seen in Kanab. Their hearts were racing, but their fear had subsided and morphed into a passionate state of adrenaline fueled excitement and justice seeking righteousness. They gazed at each other, and both felt that the other lent wings to their souls, ready to take flight, prepared to answer the call to adventure no matter the danger so long as they were together.

"Okay, we're getting that money back," she said.

Despite his recent and unexpected fright, Jim Deere fought hard to keep a smirk from spilling out across his lips. "There's no doubt in my mind," he said.

Without saying a word she sauntered into the house like a girl on a mission and when she came back to him, walking brisk and tall, her brown bandana was tied on her head and she was carrying her handbag and two helmets.

"Got the phone chargers," she said as she handed him his helmet. "You have the keys?"

His eyebrows went up. "Yeah."

Going straight over to his motorcycle and without hesitating, she stuffed her purse in one of the saddlebags. He walked toward her.

"Doin pushups, getting stronger right outside my door," he muttered under his breath.

"What?"

He shook himself awake. "Nothin."

"This can't be the end of the story with all that, 'it was I all along' stuff out of nowhere. It's so dumb it's not even funny." She stared up at him, leaning against the bike. "I will never be fooled like this again," she said, standing up slow and deliberate, running both hands down her hips. "Ready?"

Jim turned to the hay bales against the far brick wall. "We should probably take Warren's truck yeah?"

She grabbed the right handlebar of the Scout and straightened her posture, her expression a blaze of passionate confidence and sizzling sultry. "Over my dead body."

Her words caused a smirk in him and he understood something, and felt his desire for a drink dissolve from his being. His only remaining want in the world was the woman standing next to him and he saw himself climbing the heights with her, sharing thoughts with her, and relishing in beautiful and honorable things with her. It was a devotion refined beyond any grossness, a free companionship of hearts with sensation usurping fear and doubt, causing a throbbing of emotions he had never known, where feeling itself was elevated and enlightened far above the climaxes of life. He broke into a full smile and put his hand on the clutch. Drawing close with only the bike separating them, he looked openly at her with penetrating focus and uttered the words, "I love you."

Her eyes melted and widened at the same time. He tilted his head, extended forward over the saddle and kissed her slow and gentle, the gap he imagined between them now as nonexistent as the distance between their lips. They released and she gazed at him, glowing brighter than the moon.

"I know you do," she said.

Jim Deere was happy and grinned wider still, and even in the dark his eyes twinkled. He took the keys out of his pocket, put a hand on the seat and said, "You want the back right?"

Sam Diego moistened her lips with her tongue and drew her eyes upward and back down. "Umm, that depends."

"How do you mean?"

Smiling, she threw her leg over the saddle, arched her back in the front seat and buckled her helmet. Her eyes beamed as she took the keys out of his hand and fired up the bike, then with a half turn, and her fingers grasping the handlebars she revved the engine, and looking very much like her father's daughter said, "It depends if we want to catch her or not. Put your dome on!"

He sat down behind her and wrapped his arms tight around her waist as they took off down the gravel road into the night. He knew he ought to feel sick to his stomach, but he didn't. He felt simultaneously free and helpless, much like his hair blowing wildly beneath his helmet against the backdrop of the diamond studded sky. There was nothing he could do but hold on and watch the black trees fly by like shadows, with unflinching and unbreakable faith that the woman in front of him knew what she was doing.

*"And they still go where they want to
and they will be who they will be
cause there are no walls around their hearts
on the street of dreams."*
-Bill Miller

*"There's a place on a blank stretch of road
where nobody travels and nobody goes
and the deskman says these days 'round here
two young folks could probably up and disappear
into rustlin' sheets, a sleepy corner room
into the musty smell of wilted flowers
and lazy afternoon hours
at the Moonlight Motel."*
-Bruce Springsteen

*"Hey brothers, we must ride with the pride of
Chief Joseph have the courage of Geronimo
for this trail, it's long, so you have to be strong
just to find your way back home
we can find America down the trail of freedom
ride the way of my fathers from sea to sea
can you find America, hear the drums of freedom?
gonna find it together, ride this trail with me."*
-Bill Miller

## TOM SPARKS

**PUFFBIRD CLASSICS Hawi, HI**

*Quotes by: Lucinda Williams, Rosanne Cash, Redrum MC, Redspirit MC, Bruce Springsteen and Bill Miller. Poem by Bob Dylan, raid music by Phil Collins.*

Made in the USA
Coppell, TX
21 June 2021

57793922R10164